Praise for *Free Nancy Esting*

There's something delightfully engrossing about Fred Beshid's crazy, original book. The witty repartee in *Free Nancy Esting* is unfailingly intelligent and thought-provoking. In this dialogue novel, opposites repel and attract, and in so doing reveal unexpected truths about science and the soul.

—**Héctor Tobar,** author of *The Barbarian Nurseries* and *Our Migrant Souls*

"Daring, hilarious, and more than a little perceptive about the boxes us humans trap ourselves in."

—**Chip Jacobs,** bestselling author of *Arroyo* and *Smogtown*

"Nancy and Spencer's captivating meet-cute mind-meld scientifically proves opposites attract!"

—**Paula Johnson,** author of *Flash Flood*

"Whether they are discussing stardust or awkwardness, *Free Nancy Esting* explores living ourselves alive from our form and hearts rather than our analytical minds, and how we wish to live out our days. It is amusing, full of gentle wisdom, wry and will leave you feeling like—no, knowing—that you have been in the presence of something beautiful and fleeting-lasting. Mr. Beshid's light touch throughout is elegance itself."

—**Katayoon Zandvakili,** author of *Deer Table Legs*

AN UNNAMED PRESS / RARE BIRD JOINT PRODUCTION

Published in North America by the Unnamed Press.

www.unnamedpress.com

Unnamed Press, and the colophon, are registered trademarks of Unnamed Media LLC.

Paperback original ISBN: 978-1-951213-92-3
EBook ISBN: 978-1-951213-94-7
LCCN: 2023939889

Cover design and typeset by Jaya Nicely

Manufactured in the United States of America

Distributed by Publishers Group West

First Edition

Free Nancy Esting

a novel

~~Fred Beshid~~

Fred Beshid (signature)

un

LOS ANGELES, CA

To my muse

Free
Nancy
Esting

May 15

I THINK MY DATE IS A NO-SHOW. I'm sitting here by the window watching for her. She's late, so I order a latte. She's a half hour late. Why do I say *late*? She's probably flaking on me. There should be a law against this. Breach of contract. What's the appropriate punishment? I'm beginning to think no one wants to date a private investigator. It's an occupational hazard. It seems so glamorous on TV, noticing weird details about people. Nobody wants to be analyzed. It could be worse. My friend Bill is a mortician. He gets zero dates. At least I get some dates. We should form a support group. Seriously, I'll talk to him about it.

I feel like this would be a good time to begin a journal. I need a distraction. My intent is to sharpen my powers of observation, so I'm documenting what goes on around me. I remember reading somewhere that recording observations sharpens one's senses and memory. I'm hoping this practice will make me a better private investigator. So says my mentor. Maybe I'll get better cases than just being hired to spy on cheating spouses or insurance fraudsters. Stakeouts are the worst.

Okay, here we go. I'm at my usual coffee joint in Pasadena, at Lake Avenue and California Boulevard. Even though it's sunny it's a bit chilly, so the place is full of folks trying to warm up with hot drinks. The man next to me stands out because he's wearing shorts with flip-flops when everyone is bundled up. Maybe he's from the Midwest, impervious to the cold after so many frigid winters. He's reading some kind of manuscript, a bundle of sheets about an inch thick. I can see the cover, but I can only make out the headline, "Martian Habitability Potentials." Sounds pretty technical. Martian? What's that about? Maybe he's a student at Caltech working on a thesis. He looks like he's in his late twenties. Maybe he's a PhD student. I wish he'd talk to someone so I could eavesdrop.

I feel a tap on my shoulder. I'm thinking it's my date, but no. It's a stranger. She wears a sign that says VOW OF SILENCE. Intriguing. What kind of person takes a vow of silence? Silence disturbs me because it reminds me of nothingness. Awkward pauses literally make my heart pound hard in my chest. In order to prevent awkward moments from happening, I have the bad habit of interrupting someone just in case there might be a long pause. I know it's rude and a terrible way to interact. It's also a lot more work to preplan my comments. That makes me a bad listener. It's bad, I know. I'm trying to change. Self-awareness is the first step, right?

Anyway, she is tall, thin, and has a confident air about her. Oddly, she is wearing a dark blue bathrobe with a leotard underneath that matches her pale skin tone. She appears naked underneath the bathrobe, which I assume is the point. Maybe she just came from a yoga or dance class. Her makeup is dramatic, dark circles around her eyes with bright red lipstick. Like an art deco–era starlet. She is ethnically ambiguous, maybe multiracial. Early twenties. Androgynous comes to mind. She hands me a slip of paper that reads *May I share your table?* I'm tempted because I want to know more about her vow of silence, but I'm still hoping my date will show up. I tell her I'm waiting for someone. She shrugs, gives a slight bow, turns around, and scans the room for a free seat. The place is packed.

She snatches the slip of paper from my hand and presents it to the Caltech guy sitting at the next table. He looks confused as he stares at her sign. She points to the paper again. He seems irritated at the intrusion and shakes his head. He says no and points to all the stuff on the table: "Sorry. There's no room for you." She hands him another note. I'm unable to read it from where I sit. He hangs his head for a second and starts clearing the table for her. I wish I knew what the note said. What did she say to convince him to give up his table. He explains to her that he's studying and doesn't want to be disturbed. She nods and points to her sign. Vow of silence.

She sits quietly for a few minutes staring at his thesis, taking tiny sips of her coffee. I continue to watch her, hoping something happens, because I want to know more about her. Why is she wearing a bathrobe? She looks like she wants to speak. Finally, she says something about aliens. This really gets my attention because I'm a huge sci-fi fan. He looks up, confused, and asks why she is speaking. He points to her sign. I sense a conversation is starting. It appears I got my wish. I have a feeling it's going to be interesting, so I decide to turn on my recorder and slide it toward them, being careful not to draw attention. The following is my attempt to reconstruct their conversation from the recording:

—You're reading about aliens?

[He looks at the cover of his thesis with confusion.]

—If you must know, I'm writing a thesis on Martian habitability potentials, not aliens.

—Not aliens? But it says *Martians*.

—What happened to your vow of silence?

—I'm more interested in aliens than my vow of silence.

—No, Martian habitability potentials.

—I didn't know you could study aliens in college.

—I'm not studying aliens. I'm studying Mars. Specifically Mars as a potential analog to Earth.

—So *not* aliens? What do you have against aliens?

—I study the Martian atmosphere, specifically the seasonal water vapor cycles.

—You mean like the weather?

—If you prefer that vernacular.

—So you're like a Martian weatherman?

—Not exactly.

—Well, that's boring. You should study aliens. Aliens are interesting.

[I have to agree. I too would rather hear about aliens than Martian weather.]

—Well, it's complicated. As an astrobiologist, I do search for extraterrestrial life-forms. That involves the analysis of atmospheric and geophysical conditions. Specifically, seeking conditions that can support life as we know it.

—Astrobiologist? So you study alien life-forms, but instead of looking for aliens you're studying the weather on Mars?

—Well, I just said it's complicated. Didn't I just explain this? Studying the Martian atmosphere gives us tremendous insight into the history of our own biosphere and ways to find extraterrestrial life-forms . . . if they exist.

—If they exist? Maybe when you find some aliens they could explain this stuff to you.

—Okay, if you want to find aliens, go ahead. I'm going back to my work now.

[He lifts his thesis high enough so it partly covers his face.]

—So what do you do? An *astro*-what? Space something . . .

—I work for the government. NASA. JPL specifically.

—I've heard of NASA. So what's astrobiology?

—To put it simply, it's the study of life on other planets.

—That doesn't sound simple.

—Yep, it can get pretty technical. You need a working knowledge of microbiology, astronomy, geology, and chemistry. Astrobiology is an interdisciplinary field.

—Wow, you're such a nerd.

—I don't like that term.

—Why not?

—Isn't it obvious?

—No, tell me.

—I think it's derogatory.

—No, not anymore. People call themselves nerds all the time. Art *nerd*. Science *nerd*. It's normal now. You should embrace it.

—No thanks. I still think it's derogatory.

—So, you said you're studying the water on Mars? How's that going for you?

—Martian atmosphere. I study geochemical systems to evaluate the chemical energy available in potential biological environments.

—Why? Sounds boring.

—The work I'm doing now will inform planetary science missions for the next decade.

—It sounds important when you put it that way. Less boring.

—Well, I think it's important, or I wouldn't be doing it.

—Obviously. So how did you get into all this?

—I guess it started when I was young. My dad is a doctor and an amateur astronomer. We went to the Griffith Observatory all the time. The first time I was about five, and the telescope was pointed at some distant planet. As I looked through it, I had this realization that I was just a tiny creature in a vast universe. Was I insignificant?

—I like that. That's poetic and profound.

—That feeling has stayed with me my whole life.

—So it just stuck? Being tiny?

—As I got older, I thought of more questions. What keeps all the stars and planets from falling out of the sky?

—Great question. I think about that too. Especially when the moon is big and low in the night sky. How does it stay up like that?

—Questions need answers. When I got my driver's license, my dad would let me borrow his car so I could visit the telescope on Mount Wilson, the birthplace of modern astronomy. That's where Hubble figured out Andromeda is a galaxy. Just one of billions of galaxies.

—That was nice of him. He sounds supportive.

—Both of my parents are very supportive. I wouldn't have made it this far without them.

—Sounds like your dad was quite an influence.

—Definitely. He'd talk about how we're all made of stardust. Apparently, it left an impression on me. Everything is stardust.

—I think it's so inspiring that we're all made of stardust. Don't you?

—Everything is stardust. Fecal matter is also stardust. Do you find that inspiring?

—As a matter of fact, I do. Everything used to be something else. I love that. Everything just keeps getting recycled into something new. Everything is in transition.

—You're a strange bird.

—Speaking of birds, how did we go from stardust to animals that can question our own existence? Seems like quite a leap.

—It took a whole bunch of leaps. Evolution. It was just a matter of time. Everything is a math problem.

—You have a way of sucking the life out of things.

—I'm an astrobiologist. How's that possible? Don't you find math inspiring?

—Reducing everything down to math is not inspiring. Not everything is a math problem.

—What is inspiring to you? Apparently, not math.

—I think it's inspiring that we're made of stardust, because it shows the interconnectedness of all things.

—You should study math. It shows the interconnectedness of all things.

—Formulas give you formulaic results.

—You say that like it's a bad thing.

—Formulas give you the same answers as everybody else. That's boring. I'm an individual, and, as the ads on TV say, individual results may vary.

—I believe that's the point of math and science. Repeatable results.

—Math is just a tool to describe nature.

—Or nature is fundamentally mathematical.

—If you only look for math, then that's all you'll see.

—This debate has been going on since Plato's time, so we're not likely to resolve it.

—What's the debate?

—Plato believed that math was the underlying structure of nature.

—That's what you believe?

—Exactly. You seem to share the non-Platonic view that math is an artificial tool used to describe natural phenomena.

—I just don't see God sitting around doing math problems all day.

—If you knew math, we'd have more to talk about, like the Fibonacci sequence.

—Why would that impress me?

—The predictive power of mathematics is obvious when observing how the number of petals a flower has conforms to the Fibonacci sequence.

—So even a beautiful flower is a math problem? That's just sad.

—Math is beautiful.

—Not like a flower is beautiful.

—Have you heard of fractal geometry?

—No thanks.

—You should reconsider your math phobia. Since it's a universal language, it's an obvious choice for communication with extraterrestrial intelligence.

—Maybe I'll look into it since you put it that way. I like language.

—Are you familiar with phi? Perhaps you know it as the golden ratio.

—Oh, you mean divine proportion. It's used in art and architecture.

—Exactly, it's called the most beautiful number. The golden ratio is a math equation that was discovered thousands of years ago. Would you like me to show you the equation?

—I don't need the equation. I can see divine proportion everywhere I look.

[He pulls a sheet of paper out of his bag and writes something on it. He slides the paper over to her. I strain to see it, but I cannot make out any of the figures.]

—Phi is the solution to this quadratic equation. It's known as the most irrational number.

[She picks it up and laughs. She folds it into a paper airplane and launches it into his bag.]

—It's gibberish.

—Gibberish? It's an elegant mathematical equation. How can you not see the beauty in it?

—I see the beauty in a flower. A flower is not math. Divine proportion is not math. It existed before humans *discovered* it.

—I just wanted you to see the math behind it. You're entitled to your opinion.

—I get it. It's obvious you've been charmed by math.

—That's a problem?

—The problem is now you'll only look for ways to use math.

—Math is everywhere, so I don't see that as a shortcoming.

—Humans aren't mathematical.

—Yes, they are. Haven't you heard of predictive analytics?

—That sounds scary.

—It is scary. Algorithms are able to predict your health care, alcohol, and entertainment needs with remarkable accuracy.

—I don't want that.

—Soon, retailers will be shipping you products before you order them.

—That's creepy. All the more reason not to like math.

—Math is everywhere. You can't escape it.

—Not everything is mathematical. I prefer to be open-minded so I don't miss the interconnectedness of all things.

—Judging by your paper airplane, I see you're familiar with the mathematics of paper folding.

—No, but I do practice the ancient art of origami.

—A paper airplane is math—that is, geometry and aerodynamics.

—I'm pretty sure origami is an art form.

—Are you familiar with Haga's theorems?

—Apparently, you're not familiar with origami.

—Yes, I am. Paper folding can be used to solve some interesting math problems.

—My favorite is the paper crane, or *orizuru* in Japanese.

—What makes the crane so special?

—It's a symbol of good luck and longevity. The Japanese believe souls are carried up to the heavens on the wings of cranes.

—A ghost transportation system?

—Did you know if you fold a thousand cranes your wish will be granted? I did it once for a friend with cancer.

—Did it heal your friend?

—Of course it did. If it didn't work, it wouldn't be an ancient practice. It would've died out long ago.

—I prefer mathematics to the magical arts.

—You should study mystical poetry. It shows the interconnectedness of all things.

—If you really want to learn about the interconnectedness of all things, you should study math.

—Why not check out some poetry?

—I don't like poetry.

—That's sad. Why not?

—Poetry is too vague.

—That's why I like it.

—I'm not a fan of ambiguity.

—I'm not surprised.

—I like it when there's a single right answer.

—Like in math?

—Exactly.

—I feel sorry for people who don't like ambiguity.

—Why?

—There's no escaping ambiguity. It's everywhere.

—That's doesn't mean I have to like it. In fact, if I recall correctly, the human brain is hardwired with an aversion to ambiguity.

—We are not bound by our biology. At least I'm not.

—Perhaps.

—Okay, moving on. Do you think about where we came from?

—All the time. Astrobiology is the study of how stardust becomes life.

—How did we get here?

—Perhaps we hitched a ride on a meteorite.

—Maybe we're all aliens?

—Perhaps.

—Are we alone in the universe?

—Not sure, there are varying hypotheses on that subject. What do you think?

—If I had to guess, I'd say I was an alien.

—Aliens again? Okay, so that's my job in a nutshell. I'll get back to my thesis now.

[He lifts his thesis up again.]

—Wait, so what's your thesis about?

—I told you. Martian atmosphere. Not aliens.

—I know, but what are you looking for on Mars?

—I'm not sure I can discuss it in layman's terms.

—Lay*person*.

—Sorry, layperson's terms.

—Try me.

—I analyze the Mars surface for habitability and bio-signatures.

—You already lost me.

—Okay, okay. *Habitability* is a planet's potential to develop and sustain life.

—Got it. Are you trying to figure out if we could live there?

—Yes, potentially. We're looking for potential Earth analog systems. Perhaps Mars can support life as we know it.

—Well? Can it?

—Perhaps. That's what we're trying to figure out. We've found evidence of hydrothermal systems—that is, water. Now we're searching for evidence of microscopic life-forms such as bacteria.

—So you need a Martian microscope?

—Exactly. We're looking for biosignatures.

—What's a biosignature?

—Sorry, traces of past life. Think of it as a molecular fossil, or chemical evidence of past life. Is that simple enough?

—Sure, but it's a big planet. How do you know where to look?

—Anywhere that looks like it was formed by flowing water, like a riverbed.

—Oh, that's what those rovers do? They dig in the dirt?

—Yes, they excavate soil samples.

—So, is it like Earth?

—From what we can extrapolate from the layering of minerals in Martian riverbeds, primordial Mars seems similar to primordial Earth.

—Primordial? I know that term.

—You probably learned the term *primordial soup* in school.

—No, I go to a primordial sound meditation every Monday night.

—I don't know what that means.

—It's an ancient meditation practice where you chant *om* as a group.

—*Om*? Why?

—*Om* is the primordial sound that created the universe, you know, the cosmic vibration. Chanting connects your individual vibration to Oneness. Everything is connected.

—Did a guru in Santa Monica invent this?

—No, silly. It's in the Upanishads, the Sanskrit spiritual teachings. Haven't you heard of Hinduism?

—Of course. I have Indian colleagues.

—So, are you looking for life on other planets?

—Yes, I just explained that. Mars has a relatively hostile environment, so it's not exactly an Earth analog, so we're looking at other exoplanets.

—So there are other planets like Earth? Maybe they have humans on them!

—You mean potentially habitable planets? Yes, there are billions of Earthlike planets orbiting stars just within the Milky Way galaxy. The Kepler space telescope discovered many interesting planets that we're studying. I'm particularly interested in Kepler-22b. It even orbits a star that's similar to ours in size and age.

—Our sun is a star. I like that.

—Yes, that distance means that there's a chance liquid water might exist on its surface. The presence of liquid water would raise the odds that it harbors Earthlike life.

—Well, that sounds exciting. When are we going there?

—Ha! It's six hundred light-years away!

—That sounds pretty far.

—At current spacecraft speeds, it would take approximately a million years to get there.

—Yikes! So you need to find a shortcut, like a wormhole or a portal or something.

—Sure, why not?

—So you don't do that? You don't get into the wormhole stuff.

—No, theoretical physicists are into weird stuff like that.

—You're searching for aliens—that's not weird?

—I'm not searching for aliens. I'm analyzing Mars for habitability potentials. It's very straightforward.

[He taps the cover of his thesis for emphasis.]

—Theoretical physics is not straightforward?

—No, it's speculation. It's all conjecture, you know, thought experiments.

—What's a thought experiment?

—It's a hypothetical scenario that facilitates the pondering of theoretical consequences.

—Wow, that's a mouthful.

—Have you heard of Schrödinger's cat?

—Is that where there's a cat in a box and it's alive *and* dead or something?

—Close enough. That's probably the most famous example. If you want to think about quantum superposition— that is, how quantum particles can exist in two places at once—look it up.

—That seems really bizarre. What's the point?

—That is the point. The purpose of a thought experiment is to reveal flaws in our thinking, contradictions in our logic, so we can address them.

—I'll have to look that up.

—I think you'll like it. It's a brilliant illustration of how bizarre quantum theory is.

—So you don't like thought experiments?

—Not interested.

—Why not?

—Too abstract.

—Too vague? Like poetry?

—Exactly. For instance, given that we can safely assume the observable universe contains trillions of galaxies, and assuming space-time is infinite, then at some point repetition is inevitable because particles can only be arranged in a finite number of ways. What do you think?

—That gives me a headache.

—Me too.

[Me too. I can't imagine sitting around thinking about stuff like that all day.]

—My job is to simply collect and analyze data.

—And extrapolate? I like that word.

—Yes, I've been known to extrapolate.

[They both laugh.]

—So you tell NASA where to land the rockets on Mars?

—Yes, I'm part of a team that chooses targets, or landing sites.

—That's cool. So you prefer to measure stuff.

—Sure, you could say that.

—So have you found any evidence of life on Mars?

—Not exactly. We've found evidence of water on Mars, but proof of life has been elusive so far. High levels of radiation might have destroyed organic molecules on the surface. So I'm not expecting to find any biosignatures just yet. I'm hoping there are chemotrophs below the surface.

—Chemotrophs? What's that?

—They're organisms that obtain energy from chemical reactions, similar to bacteria and fungi.

—Wait, do we have those here?

—Of course. Look around some lava beds or deep-sea thermal vents.

—I'll get right on that.

—Oh, also, there's methane in the atmosphere, which may be a biosignature.

—So you think life just appears out of nowhere?

—The origin of life? You mean abiogenesis versus panspermia?

—Huh?

—Abiogenesis is a theory that states that life arose here via spontaneous means from nonliving matter. Versus panspermia, that life transferred here from somewhere else.

—Interesting. I think about this stuff, but I had no idea these ideas had names.

—Feel free to read about it.

—I'll have to look that up.

[She points to his thesis.]

—So what's all this? It's not finished yet?

—Well, this is my doctoral dissertation. Yes, it's finished, but I still need to defend it.

—Wait. You have to defend your homework? Are they going to attack you?

—Yes, sort of. My research adviser and the thesis committee will try to poke holes in my theories and my supporting evidence. It's called a dissertation defense.

—They sound mean. That doesn't sound very supportive. [He laughs.]

—It's an honor to have them critique my work. How else can I improve?

—That's true, but maybe they can be nicer. Less hostile. More supportive.

—Criticism is part of the process. A scientist practices the scientific method. He or she observes, formulates a hypothesis, conducts experiments to test the hypothesis, and publishes the findings so it can be peer-reviewed.

—I see. So you want criticism?

—Yes. Why?

—Most people don't want criticism. They only want validation.

—Really? Then how would I discover potential flaws in my reasoning?

—So they just grill you and you have to have all the answers?

—That's an oversimplification of the process, but accurate.

—So a good dissertation has all the answers?

—Well, a good dissertation should answer questions but should also suggest more questions for further research.

—That's good. I love questions. Answers destroy questions.

—I guess that's one way of looking at it.

—So basically your job is to impress these people?

—Yes, I guess so.

—I'd rather be bewildered than clever.

—Well, I'm not sure I'd want to discourage cleverness.

—Of course not, you're in the cleverness business.

—What's wrong with being clever?

—Cleverness is about impressing others. That's how you lose yourself.

—I'm hoping my cleverness will earn me a PhD. That's a gain, not a loss.

—Yes, like I said, you're in the cleverness business. We're social animals, so we give up parts of ourselves to get approval and love.

—As social animals we are defined by social structures. We need to fit in in order to survive.

—Yeah, I don't like that.

—It's hardwired in us. We're social animals. You can't change that.

—Ha! I already have.

—You're an enigma.

—Thank you. Thanks for noticing.

—That's a compliment?

—I take everything as a compliment.

—I wish I could do that.

—It just takes practice. Now, if you'll excuse me, I'm due in the little ladies' room.

[As she walks toward the restroom, he returns to his thesis until he is interrupted by her return.]

—So where were we? Were we talking about aliens?

—I think we were finished with extraterrestrials.

—Not quite. So we agree alien life is possible. There are billions of stars out there, so it seems likely there are some other creatures out there, yes?

—You'd like the astrobiological Copernican principle.

—What's that?

—It states that terrestrial life is not special, so what happened here can happen anywhere.

—I like that. Maybe we're not so special. We're just ordinary life-forms doing our thing.

—Perhaps. Or we could be unique.

—But maybe you're looking for the wrong things.

—How so?

—Maybe everything is alive.

—That's one theory. Panpsychism.

—That has a name?

—Yes.

—I'll have to look that up.

—As a self-respecting scientist, I'd prefer not to investigate the nature of consciousness.

—Because you can't measure it?

—That's part of it.

—Does this mean you won't look for aliens?

[He opens his thesis and points to her sign.]

—The only reason I let you sit here is because you were wearing a sign that says VOW OF SILENCE. I mistakenly thought you would not disturb me.

—I'm sorry I misled you. I only wear it to discourage people from talking to me.

—I need a sign like that.

—I'm not a big fan of people in general. They interrupt my thoughts.

—I know exactly how you feel.

—I usually wear a poncho, but I'm wearing my work clothes right now.

[He closes his thesis again. He looks resigned.]

—Poncho? Why?

—You know, to hide my hands so people don't touch them.

—Touch them? Oh, you mean shaking hands.

—I don't want strangers touching my hands.

—That's a good idea.

—It creates awkward situations. I like that.

—You like awkward situations?

—Yes. Don't you?

—No. It seems most people go to great lengths to avoid feeling awkward.

—I know. That's why I like it.

—Why?

—Awkwardness reveals true character.

—That puzzles me.

—Good, maybe you'll grow a little.

—But if you're trying to avoid people, why not just stay home?

—My roommate is a sex addict.

—Say no more. Spare me the details.

—Also, my neighbor plays the cello. I can hear it even with earplugs.

—Actually, that sounds pleasant. I enjoy classical music.

—She also writes letters on a vintage typewriter.

—That sounds unpleasant. People still own typewriters?

—Yep, they're hip now. You know, like vinyl.

—Vinyl? Oh, you mean records.

—Yep, it's hip.

—I wouldn't know. I don't follow trends.

—My life has a soundtrack. It's confusing when her music doesn't go with my mood.

—I see. Perhaps she'll move?

—Never. She'll never leave.

—Why are you so convinced?

—She's trying to get married, but she has an antidowry.

—*Antidowry*? What's that?

—So you know how a dowry works?

—In traditional cultures it's the groom's compensation to the bride's parents.

—Yep, but in her case she has an antidowry. She has half a million dollars in student loans from the music conservatory. She says no one will marry her with that much debt.

—I see. Perhaps you'll have an opportunity to move out then.

—Maybe. So that's why I'm here bugging you.

—Lucky me.

—So, why are you here?

—Chatty roommates.

—Chatty? What do they talk about? Celebrity gossip?

—Theoretical physics.

—Ugh, that sounds like hell. Wait, I thought you like physics and stuff.

—Yes, but there's a limit. I think they suffer from too much conjecture.

—Sounds serious.

—I'm afraid to ask, but . . .

—Ask away!

—Well . . . why are you wearing a bathrobe?

—Why not?

—Well, previously you said you were wearing your *work* clothes.

[She laughs aloud and covers her mouth.]

—So you're dying to know what my job is? Take a guess.

—I'd rather not.

—Take a guess.

—How about a clue?

—I work for the government, just like you.

—Really? I have no idea.

—Guess. I'll give you a hint: I stand around doing nothing.

—You do nothing? In a bathrobe?

—Exactly. Nothing.

—Security guard?

—Wow, that's a great guess. But in a bathrobe?

—Are you a spy?

—I'm not a spy, but I like your creativity.

—More clues, please.

—Creativity! That's your clue.

—Huh? So we have bathrobe, standing around, and creativity? I have no idea.

—Well, actually, when I'm working I take the bathrobe off.

—What?

—You heard me.

—I'm not playing your game anymore.

—Come on. I'll give you another clue: I work for the college.

—You're not a professor.

—Not a professor, but you're getting closer. I stand around and do nothing.

—And taxpayers pay you for this?

—Yep. I'm worth every cent.

—I give up.

—No more guesses?

—To be honest, I don't like games. I was just trying to humor you.

—Artist model.

—Artist model?

—Artist model. That's my official government job title.

—Forgive my ignorance. I don't even know what that is.

—I pose nude for art classes. Sometimes I wear a nude leotard like this one if I'm working with younger kids, like at the arts magnet.

[She opens the top of her bathrobe to reveal a leotard that matches her skin tone.]

—No clothes? As in naked? Wow, I can't think of any other government job that requires being naked.

—No, not naked. I'm *nude*! Grow up.

[He looks around the room as if embarrassed, but no one seems to notice.]

—Not naked? I'm sorry . . . I'm not . . . Could you please explain the distinction?

—*Naked* means you're without clothes. *Nude* means you're not supposed to have clothes.

—I see. Interesting distinction. Something I never would have considered.

—Isn't learning fun?

—Wow, so . . . standing in front of strangers with no clothes, getting stared at, and . . .

—I stare back sometimes. Humans rarely get an opportunity to stare at one another.

—That's true.

—You should try it.

—Staring at people?

—No, posing nude.

—No thanks. I have nightmares about that.

—You underestimate yourself.

—Perhaps. How long do these poses last?

—Well, let's see. There's a warm-up pose that's two to five minutes. Longer poses are fifteen to thirty minutes.

—Wow, thirty minutes. I can't imagine holding still for that long.

—Painters and sculptors need the longer poses. Drawing instructors prefer the shorter poses.

—So how long is a class?

—A typical session is three hours. Sometimes we'll use one pose for the whole session, with breaks, of course, every ten minutes or so.

—Isn't it uncomfortable?

—Of course it is! The more interesting the pose, the more painful it is.

—Give me an example of a challenging pose so I can picture it.

—All my weight on one leg and holding my arms above my heart.

[She places her hands on her head.]

—I see. The blood drains from your arms. That's the problem.

—You have to respect your limitations. You're fighting gravity.

—I work for the space program, so I know about fighting gravity.

[He laughs to himself.]

—Oh, yeah. You know gravity.

—Do you enjoy the suffering?

—No. I'm not afraid of pain, but I prefer not to suffer. Why? That's an odd question.

—It seems a lot of artists enjoy suffering. Is that a stereotype? Like it makes them a better artist. Perhaps it makes life more meaningful.

—Not true. Artists and scientists are similar in many ways.

—How so? I don't see it.

—They both tend to ask a lot of questions.

—Perhaps. So . . . with the posing . . . you're not embarrassed?

—This is why I don't like to tell people what I do for a living. It leads to a lot of embarrassing questions.

—I apologize. Am I embarrassing you?

—No, you're embarrassing *yourself*.

[He lets out a nervous laugh.]

—So *you're* not embarrassed?

—Shame? No. It's not like I get heckled or groped. I feel safe. It's a controlled environment.

—So it's purely an academic exercise.

—Exactly.

—Sorry, my only point of reference for public nudity is a strip club.

—No, no. That's very different . . . different context . . . different purpose.

—Well, people are paying to see your nude body?

—You make it sound like *prostitution*.

—Have I embarrassed myself again?

—Yes. Let's just say you have to be comfortable with your body. I get paid for being who I am, and that's rare.

—Really? Doesn't everyone get paid for being who they are?

—Most people get paid to act like somebody else.

—Like actors?

—Most people are pretending to be something they are not.

—Perhaps. Was it always easy for you?

—It was weird at first, but I got used to it.

—So it was awkward at first. But wait, you said you like awkward situations.

—I like awkwardness in others.

—I see.

—Also, the skeleton incident was traumatizing.

—Skeleton incident?

—I was standing there, frozen in a pose, and the instructor told the students to draw my skeleton. I had never thought about having a skeleton inside me before. I had to stand there for five minutes thinking about my skeleton while a class full of students drew it. It was creepy. I almost had a panic attack.

—Really? I think about that all the time. I'm fascinated by human biology.

—I guess that makes sense as a biologist.

—So learning human anatomy must be important to artists, since they go to all this trouble.

—Oh, yes. That's the foundation of art education. Understanding human anatomy helps us understand our relationship to the world.

—I can see the value in learning about how our bodies function.

—It's fundamental.

—So the students are never inappropriate?

—Rarely.

—So there was an incident?

—Well, one time, I finished a pose, put on my robe, and sat down on my stool to rest. I was checking the messages on my phone, and when I looked up I noticed one of the students was trying to look up my robe. It was odd. The student had just stared at my nude body for twenty minutes but still couldn't resist sneaking a peek up my robe.

—I share your confusion. Well, I guess men are curious creatures.

—I didn't say it was a man.

—Oh, oh . . . I see.

—I have a confession.

—Am I about to be embarrassed again?

—No, it's your job to embarrass yourself, not mine.

—So, what is it?

—I get paid to do *nothing*, but I'm actually doing *something*.

—I was wondering how you pass the time. What goes on in your mind while you pose?

—Thinking. I think a lot.

—About what?

—I can't speak for other models, but I get superconscious.

—You mean like psychic?

—I don't like that term. I prefer *superconscious*.

—Fine.

—Anyway, everything seems more alive. I can hear other people's thoughts. I feel like I can direct the artistic activities in the studio.

—Wow, that sounds like a nightmare. I wouldn't want that kind of awareness.

—That's because you're not a muse.

—So you're a *muse*?

—Yes. You have something against muses?

—I don't like the idea of spirits controlling my mind.

—Muses don't control you. We make suggestions. You have free will.

—What's the point then?

—Just because you're given a brilliant idea doesn't mean you have to act on it. I help artists collaborate with the universe. I'm just a guide and a channel.

—So you're saying I have free will. That's reassuring.

—There are muses for science too. Maybe you already have one?

—No thanks. I enjoy my independence.

—Suit yourself.

—So you inspire the production of artistic works?

—Exactly. I inspire creative thoughts and ways of seeing one would not normally see. *Inspire* means *to breathe life into*. Cool, huh?

—And what happens to these ideas that you submit but are not acted upon?

—That's a really good question. I'm not sure. Maybe they go back into the ether for someone else to use?

—So you have no interest in the outcome?

—I have no attachment to what happens. I'm not in charge.

—I see. Do you inspire confidence too?

—Confidence is overrated.

—Confidence is bad?

—No, just overrated.

—Huh?

—Insecurity is good.

—What? Why?

—Insecurity inspires improvement.

—Interesting viewpoint.

—Do you have a problem with insecurity?

—Not that I know of, but it is something I consider. I mean . . . I guess I do occasionally have my doubts.

—How so?

—I often wonder if my insecurities are unsubstantiated.

—Sounds like you need the guidance of a muse.

—I'm fine. But I thought muses were incarnate beings that lived in museums.

—Normally they do, but we've expanded our horizons. The people in museums are already cultured, so they don't need muses. That's easy pickings.

—I guess it would be more challenging and gratifying to work with students.

—Exactly. That's where it's needed most. You're a student. Are you sure you don't want a muse?

—No thanks. I think it's counterproductive to externalize creativity in that way.

—Really? Where do you think your ideas come from?

—From me! They're *my* ideas. I think them up all by myself. I don't believe I'm controlled by external forces.

—The ancient Greeks believed ideas came from spirits called muses. Artists weren't special; they were simply copying nature.

—Yes, I know that, but I don't believe in spirits.

—I'm not surprised. Probably because you can't see them.

—Sure, that's as good a reason as any.

—So when the Renaissance came along, artists started taking credit for their creations . . .

—I'm somewhat familiar with art history.

—So your Martian paper there is filled with *your* ideas. That's what you think?

—Yes, that's the whole point of this exercise.

—Getting credit seems very important to you.

—Of course. Don't you care about getting credit for your work?

—I create art through others. I don't care about credit.

—So the artist gets credit and you don't care?

—You can get a lot more done if you don't care who gets the credit.

—I recall Harry Truman saying something similar.

—If you say so. Or maybe he got the idea from a muse. [He shakes his head.]

—I'm not sure if you're being serious?

—The ego interferes with learning and interesting conversations.

—You're funny. So I guess you can't have any ambitions?

—My ambition is to be ambitionless!

—That makes no sense. Isn't that a paradox?

—Yes! That's why I like it.

—Don't you feel any need to reconcile these contradictory beliefs of yours?

—Not really. No.

—Why not?

—Because that would ruin everything.

—Huh?

—I live in a world of infinite possibilities. Don't you see? When you believe in something, that closes the door to believing in something else. The only reason to shut a door is to keep something out. Why would I keep something out?

—So this is an attempt at being open-minded?

—Yes, I want to merge with everything. That's how you achieve Oneness.

—Oneness? Are you talking about mysticism?

—I guess you could call it that.

—Sorry, I'm not well versed in mysticism.

—Really? You seem to understand everything is connected.

—I assure you, I am not a mystic.

—You don't have to wake up. It's your choice to stay asleep.

—And how does one *wake up*?

—If you sit quietly long enough, it happens on its own.

—So I just sit in a cave like a hermit, and eventually I will feel connected with everything?

—Yes!

—Just sit there and do nothing? So it's that easy?

—Doing nothing is not easy.

—I don't think I need it. I already know everything is connected.

—So you *are* a mystic too?

—No, I believe all things are connected because I'm a scientist.

—That's unfortunate. You have an intellectual understanding but not a spiritual one.

—What are you getting at?

—There's a world beyond your questions and measurements.

—What does that mean?

—The goal of science is to demystify the world. What good is a world without magic?

—Not true. Questions tend to create more questions. As I said before, the point of a thesis is to inspire more inquiry.

—Mysticism is a way of exploring the mysteries of life.

—*Science* is a way of exploring the mysteries of life.

—You're on the right path. Just remember to question everything, including your own questions.

—Huh?

—If you want answers, you won't find them where you expect them.

[He shakes his head. I'm lost too.]

—This is just nonsense.

—Remember what I said about interesting conversations?

—Yes, but this is just nonsense.

—Nonsense leads to the truth.

—Okay, now I know you're just messing with me.

—Am I? How many discoveries were made by *accident*? [She makes air quotes with her fingers.]

—Are you referring to serendipity?

—Yes, looking for one thing and finding another.

—What about it?

—Lots of so-called inventions and discoveries are just accidents.

—I'm not sure that's helpful, but—

—Helpful? There is no helpful. Everything is already perfect.

—Huh? What are you saying? There's nothing wrong anywhere?

—Nope.

—Pollution? Crime? Corruption?

—The universe is self-organizing. It's in the process of working things out. Like a beehive.

—Finally, something we can agree on.

—The reason everything is the way it is now is because of everything that's happened in the past.

—You could make that argument.

—There's no reason to worry, because the universe will continue to organize itself with or without you.

—What about free will? Determinism?

—We have free will, but not as much as people think.

—That seems to be where neuroscience is headed.

—It's obvious.

—So if you're not trying to be helpful, then what are you doing?

—I introduce people to themselves.

—That's not helpful?

—No, it's disturbing to people. They *think* they know who they are, but it turns out they don't know themselves. Don't you know those around us define us?

—Sounds familiar.

—As a child you can sing, dance, and draw. No limitations. As we get older, we want approval, so we only do what we're good at.

—I'm not a psychologist, but that seems to be true.

—Being yourself is really hard. We're surrounded by people who want us to forget who we are: parents, advertisers, religions, governments, employers. They all want us to be someone else. How can we ignore all these messages?

—So this is what you think about while you model?

—Our consumer economy hammers us with messages to consume. What if I don't want to be a consumer? What if I want to be a producer? Or neither?

—And why are you so consumed by this? No pun intended.

—Being yourself inspires others to do the same. What's more important than that?

—Personally, I think science and technology are more important.

—I don't think technology will save us.

—I wouldn't be so quick to discount technology. Traditionally humans have been shaped by their environment, but now humans shape the environment.

—More like *destroy* the environment.

—I'm an optimist when it comes to our technological potential.

—I'm a realist.

—So what's the alternative to science? Religion?

—Believing technology will save us blinds us to other possibilities.

—And what exactly are those possibilities?

—Not sure. Technology is only good if it brings more kindness into the world.

—That'll be challenging in a culture based on the myth of progress.

—Myth of progress?

—It's the idea that the human condition will continue to improve.

—What does *progress* even mean? For who? What are we progressing toward?

—Good question. Now we're getting into questions of values, which science is not equipped to handle.

—True. We need a poet or philosopher.

—Or an ethicist.

—For the record, I'm not against science. I just think it's a work in progress like everything else in the universe.

—Agreed. Science can improve lives, but we don't always agree on what needs improving.

—What does *improvement* even mean?

—That's true. That's a question of values.

—Exactly. Science also destroys lives. Is the atomic bomb good? Is the internet good? Half the world doesn't have access to a toilet and the other half can't put their phone down. Is that good or bad?

—How should I know? I'm just an astrobiologist.

—You don't think about this stuff? What if you find life on Mars? Will that be *progress*?

—Like I said, science can't answer those questions because they are value driven.

—I'm just saying.

—I'm well aware of the limitations of science. For example, we don't even know how eels reproduce.

—Really? That seems odd. Don't they lay eggs?

—We assume they spawn, but we can't seem to find any eel eggs.

—For thousands of years we've looked to the sky for answers, and we've invented all kinds of interesting technology to help us. Where has it gotten us?

—Okay, okay. I get it. You're not a fan of technology.

—I just wish we were as good at spreading kindness as we are at monetizing things.

—Point taken.

—Humanity will die from progress.

—Meaning?

—Every solution is a problem.

—Meaning?

—For anything gained something is lost. We've sold our humanity to buy convenience.

—Perhaps it was worth it. Who gets to decide?

—You're looking for other planets that humans can live on. Do humans deserve another planet? I'm mean, look at what we've done to this one. Won't humans just ruin the new planet too? Ever since ancient history we've been destroying this planet. After we hunted whales into extinction, we started drilling for oil. Who cut down the last tree on Easter Island?

—Wow, that's really cynical.

—Is it?

—I'm optimistic.

—Every solution is a problem. I'm just reporting the facts.

—Suggesting there's no hope for humanity seems rather pessimistic.

—Well, look at you. You're looking for a new home for the human race. Isn't that pessimistic?

—Good point.

—I've heard it said that everything contains within it the seeds of its own destruction.

—That's the cycle of life.

—I guess so.

—Maybe you're right. The forecast for our planet is pretty bleak. Our sun is about halfway through its life. It only has about five billion years left before its hydrogen is used up. It'll explode into a red giant, then shrink into a white dwarf, vaporizing Earth in the process.

—Yikes!

—Don't worry, it's a billion years away. We won't be around then.

—Why are you so sure? Haven't you heard of reincarnation?

—Yes, but I don't believe in it.

—Just because you don't believe in it doesn't mean you won't be reincarnated.

—Now that I think about it, *Homo sapiens* aren't the only species that has the potential to destroy its own environment.

—I'm sorry to hear that.

—In fact, you've probably enjoyed a product made by environmental destruction.

—What are you talking about?

—Do you enjoy wine?

—Occasionally.

—The alcohol in wine is a waste product of the yeast colony. It's part of a metabolic process called fermentation. Given enough glucose is present, the yeast will continue to produce alcohol until the concentration reaches approximately fifteen percent. The toxicity of the ethanol ends the metabolic cycle of the yeast colony.

—So they unknowingly kill themselves, and then we get wine?

—Isn't science fun?

—Why do you know things like this?

—I have a master's degree in microbial ecology.

—That doesn't answer my question.

—I think it does.

—Anyway, I'm not a pessimist. Like the mystic says, if the world ends while you're planting flowers, keep planting. I'm just saying we don't need more technology. We need more kindness. How is that cynical?

—Not when you present it in that fashion.

—Okay, good. Something to think about.

—Is this what you think about while you model?

—Changing the subject, are we? Are you interested in thinking?

—Yes, I'm fascinated by metacognition.

—What's that?

—Thinking about thinking.

—Isn't that supposed to be unique to humans?

—Yes, as far as we know.

—I think about life and the universe. The big questions.

—Like what?

—Why do humans like kissing when other animals don't?

—How do you know other animals don't like to kiss?

—I thought that was common knowledge.

—Is it? Perhaps it's because we have sucking mouth parts. That's rare for mammals.

—In the ancient Sanskrit scriptures, they describe kissing as inhaling each other's soul. I love that.

—Something to think about.

—Here's another big question: What do dogs dream about?

—What makes you think dogs dream?

—I had a dog that would whine and twitch his legs while he was sleeping.

—Perhaps he was dreaming about being chased.

—Can I ask you a question? I mean, as a biologist?

—Do I have to answer as a biologist?

—Yes.

—Well?

—Are humans supposed to be vegetarian?

—Supposed to? That sounds like a question of values, so I can't answer it.

—Sorry, maybe I asked it wrong. I want a scientific answer.

—Okay, humans are omnivores. We can consume everything from vegetation to other animals. Also, other autotrophs like algae and fungi. Oh, and insects. Our long intestines, diverse dentition, and binocular vision facilitate this variety of consumption.

—Thank you. That was very scientific sounding.

—I should hope so.

—But you didn't answer the question.

—You're asking are we *supposed* to be vegetarians? Isn't that a leading question?

—Maybe.

—Have you heard of anthropocentrism?

—No, should I?

—It's a belief that considers humans to be superior to all other life-forms; therefore, humans are justified in exploiting other animals.

—That's disgusting!

—It's a common assumption in many Western religions and belief systems.

—So you think we're supposed to be vegetarians?

—Our eyes are in front of our skulls. We have the same binocular visual system as a tiger or a wolf.

—What does that mean?

—That means we're predators. We are hunters.

—But I don't want to be a predator.

—Well, you have to *kill* something in order to survive.

—I'm a vegetarian.

—Herbivory is a type of predation.

—Well, I can't eat meat.

—Why do you find carnivory so objectionable?

—Because when I eat meat I can hear the animal complaining inside me.

—Okay . . . well, that's beyond the scope of science.

—Do you have that problem?

—No, my food does not talk to me. Fortunately, I lack that kind of awareness.

—I see. That kind of awareness should only be developed gradually, so you're prepared for it. Everything is part of our evolution.

—So you believe in evolution?

—Of course. We're growing and evolving right now. That's the human experiment that leads us to union with God, Oneness.

—If you say so.

—So we both agree we are still evolving?

—Sure, perhaps we're evolving into crabs. We're the result of countless genetic mutations.

—We're mutations? That doesn't sound good. That sounds horrible. We're mutants!

—I'm not sure if it's good or bad, but I know it's happening.

—Sure, maybe we'll get better. Maybe humans will become more kind and joyful. Wouldn't that be great?

—Sure, or maybe we'll evolve into crabs.

—Speaking of that, I read this article about how they found these giant turtles that were like thirty million years old. They were huge, like the size of a car, but now turtles are way smaller. Do you think every species is evolving into a smaller version of itself?

—I can't be certain, as that's not my field of expertise. It's an interesting theory and certainly possible.

—But didn't dinosaurs evolve into birds?

—I believe researchers of comparative genomics have concluded that the closest modern species to that of the *Tyrannosaurus rex* is the chicken.

—No way! That's more evidence that all species are shrinking.

—It's possible.

—Do you think in a million years that humans will be the size of squirrels?

—You're funny. Will humans have to compete with rodents for food in the future?

—No, silly. Squirrels would then be the size of mice.

—Of course, how silly of me.

—Do you ever feel like you're the wrong species?

—I don't know what that means.

—I don't know either.

—Can we get back to your modeling?

—Sure.

—Do you find it empowering?

—No, why do you ask?

—I've heard strippers say that.

—I'm not a stripper. Stop bringing that up.

—Sorry, I didn't mean to imply that.

—Besides what do you know about strippers?

—Richard Feynman enjoyed strippers.

—Who?

—Richard Feynman? Surely you must have heard of him.

—No, why? Is he famous?

—He's quite well-known. My professor showed me his book of nude drawings. He liked to hang out at a local strip club and draw the dancers.

—Never heard of him. If he were a famous artist, I would know him.

—Well, he wasn't a famous artist. At least not that I'm aware of.

—Famous for what then?

—Quantum physics. Haven't you heard of QED? Feynman received the 1965 Nobel Prize in Physics for his work in quantum electrodynamics.

—Sorry, doesn't ring a bell.

—So you have no interest in electromagnetic fields? Or particle physics?

—What do you think?

—I don't want to assume.

—And yet you do.

—Anyway, he liked *nude* women.

—What's not to like?

—So I went to see strippers because Feynman enjoyed them.

—Did you *enjoy* it?

—Not really. It made me uncomfortable.

—You're probably more comfortable exposing your insides.

—Oh, you mean intellectually. I guess you're right.

[He stares down at his thesis.]

—After all, that's what a thesis is. It's a type of showing off.

[They both laugh.]

—I guess you're right.

—A thesis is more tolerable than a guitar solo.

—Perhaps. I see your point.

—I don't like guitar solos.

—So you don't get nervous?

—No, catching spiders in the bathtub makes me nervous. Everything else is about keeping your cool.

—True.

—So many people look in the mirror and dislike what they see. It's sad.

—And you don't?

—I don't like it or dislike it. I don't feel a need to judge my looks. Besides, it's just a temporary home.

—Okay, on that note I guess I'll return to my work now.

—Wait. Did you study quantum physics?

—My undergrad degree is in physics with a focus on quantum physics. Why?

—I believe in quantum physics.

—Quantum physics is not a belief system.

—Sure it is. Like attracts like. That's why I avoid negative thinking.

—I have no idea what you're talking about, but I'm sure you're not talking about science.

—Haven't you heard of *manifesting*?

—Sounds vaguely familiar.

—It's all about quantum physics.

—Manifesting is not science. It's just magical thinking.

—Now you're being negative.

—It's not a belief system.

—Sure it is. Haven't you heard of the law of attraction?

—That's new age nonsense. It's just a clever marketing ploy to sell books.

—Bad thoughts attract bad things into your life. It's a fact.

—That's not quantum physics. I'm not sure what that is.

—So you don't think negative thoughts affect our lives?

—You mean on a quantum level? No.

—That's unfortunate.

—If you say so.

—I understand quantum physics pretty well. I use it all the time when I'm manifesting.

—Who made you an expert on manifesting?

—I saw a documentary on it. I read a book too. A few books.

—I have completed extensive coursework in quantization, quantum entanglement, and wave-particle duality. I don't recall manifesting ever coming up.

—So you admit your ignorance?

—I'm naturally suspicious of anyone who claims to understand quantum mechanics. Even my professors said no one understands it.

—It's simple.

—Okay, then explain to me how radiation can exist as a particle and a wave. Isn't that a contradiction?

—I would explain it to you, but you wouldn't understand.

—Ha! That's what I thought. So do you really think you can control the universe with your mind?

—Well, when you put it that way it does sound kind of silly. I wouldn't use the word *control*.

—What then? Can you put it in a way that doesn't sound *silly*?

—Maybe *control* is not a good word. *Influence* is a better word.

—Wouldn't you say everyone has an influence on his or her environment?

—That reminds me of when I was a kid. I would be in bed at night, and when I heard dogs barking in the neighborhood I would calm them down with my mind.

—Is that a true story?

—Of course.

—Can we perform an experiment to test it?

—No, it's gone.

—Gone? Where?

—I got hit by lightning while driving in a car and lost that superpower.

—This whole story sounds fabricated.

—I know, but it's true. That's why I like it. So what's your superpower?

—I don't have one. I'm not a comic book character.

—Come on, everyone has something.

—I guess being good at math.

—That's your superpower?

—Studying physics is all about math. A single problem might take hours to solve.

—I can't believe you don't believe our minds have influence over our lives. What about placebos?

—I believe we do have some influence over ourselves, but I don't think we can control anything with our thoughts.

—So we *do* have free will?

—Of course.

—Speaking of free will, why did you quit studying the quantum stuff?

—I didn't quit. I moved on to astrobiology.

—Why not stay with the quantum stuff?

—Randomness.

—Huh?

—I'm not sure I can explain it in layman's terms, but I'll try.

—Layperson.

—Sorry. Layperson. I didn't know what to do with randomness. Particles disappear and reappear. How can I analyze a phenomenon that lacks definite properties?

—Huh?

—In the past we thought of everything as being a particle or a wave. But now quantum theory seems to suggest that matter has properties that are particle-like and wave-like.

—That's in layperson's terms?

—Okay, let me try again. Quantum mechanics attempts to predict particle behavior, but this has proved elusive. Since particle behavior appears to be random, we can only describe it in terms of probabilities. So does the lack of predictable outcomes mean there's an underlying intrinsic randomness to everything?

—Maybe. Or maybe it's not random. Maybe they choose to disappear and reappear?

—Are you suggesting particles have consciousness? Free will?

—Sure, maybe everything is alive.

—Are you referring to panpsychism?

—Didn't you mention that earlier?

—Yes.

—I'll have to look that up.

—The problem with panpsychism is that there's no way to test it empirically, so there's no direct evidence to support that theory.

—Or to *disprove* it?

—That's true. There's no evidence to disprove the theory.

—So it might be true?

—I have no idea. I'll think about it. You'd be better off discussing it with a theoretical physicist.

—How do I get one?

—Try the university.

—That's a good idea. I'll check it out.

—Anyway, quantum theory presents anomalies that can't be explained by the laws of classical physics. Even Einstein was bothered by them.

—Really? That's hard to believe. Give me an example.

—Well, let's see. Quantum entanglement is a good example. Particles like photons seem to be able to communicate with each other instantaneously over great distances. This bothered Einstein, so he called it *spooky action at a distance*.

—*Spooky*? Why *spooky*?

—He called it *spooky* because the interaction seems to happen faster than the speed of light, which, according to his theory of relativity, is not possible.

—Well, if Einstein couldn't understand it, then I'm not even going to try.

—Like I said, quantum theory is very bizarre. Have you heard of the observer effect?

—Not sure.

—The mere act of observing particles has the potential to influence them.

—Huh? I've heard of that. So particles know when someone's watching them? Like they're self-conscious?

—I wouldn't go that far. I wouldn't say particles have consciousness. We just can't predict their behavior sometimes.

—They're unpredictable? So you want particle behavior to be predictable?

—How can scientists study a phenomenon that challenges the very idea of the existence of an objective reality?

—I see your point. Maybe there is no objective reality. I can see that would be a problem for scientists, but it doesn't bother me. I'm not a big fan of objectivity.

—Ha! I can see that.

—Maybe everything is an illusion. That's what the Buddhists say.

—Maybe. There are alternate theories for everything.

—Well, I guess if we can question Einstein, we can question anything, right?

—Einstein was human. He made mistakes just like everyone else. His miscalculations regarding gravity are well-known. General relativity is a good working theory for now, but it's lacking. For example, it doesn't explain what happens inside of black holes.

—If you say so.

—I think we need more alternative theories of gravity.

—Sure, why not? Do you have any ideas?

—Well, I don't, but other scientists have proposed alternative models for gravity. For example, chameleon theory is an interesting alternative to general relativity. Teleparallel gravity sounds promising as well.

—I'm getting a headache again.

—Sorry, I got carried away.

—So, let's get back to randomness. Does randomness bother you?

—I assumed it bothers everyone. No?

—Not me. I like randomness. It means the world is alive and is still being created, which means it's still evolving.

—Perhaps. I'll have to think about it.

—I tried to sit at the table next to us, but that man refused me. But here I am with you talking about aliens. Wasn't this all random?

[She points at me. I look away, trying to hide my nervousness. Fortunately, she turns toward him again.]

—Not aliens again.

—Randomness is reality. To ignore randomness is to ignore reality.

—I'm not ignoring it. I'm just not interested in studying it.

—It there a difference?

—Yes. We can't study everything. There's too much to know.

—You should embrace randomness. Randomness is how you can overcome your programmed thinking. I use it to escape social programming, because I don't want others to define me.

—How do you do that?

—When I'm at the library I roll dice to get a random Dewey decimal code. Then I read the book that was chosen at random.

—What's the point?

—It removes my personal preferences from my choices, and that makes me aware of my tendencies in the choices I make.

—Interesting. So you don't like math, but you like the Dewey decimal system?

—You're missing the point.

—What's the point again?

—It reminds me to have a more spiritual understanding of life. This is a place where mysteries are revered rather than problems to be solved.

—Well, I'm a scientist, and randomness conflicts with deterministic laws of cause and effect.

—I'm just suggesting you question your patterned thinking. It's all social programming.

—We are pattern-seeking animals, so randomness conflicts with our instincts. Our brains are hardwired to look for patterns.

—Our brains are hardwired to do lots of things we're better off not doing.

—Ha! I can't argue with that.

—I'm glad we can agree on something.

—But maybe things are not random. Maybe that's an illusion.

—Sure, maybe particles are conscious and they decide everything.

—So, you're saying the greater consciousness is created by the trillions of conscious particles joining together?

—Why not?

—So how does the consciousness of these subatomic particles come together?

—How should I know? I'm not a scientist!

[He laughs hard.]

—All the easy problems have been solved.

—Maybe your expectation that the world be understandable and predictable might be unrealistic.

—Perhaps. But how will we know unless we try? Perhaps everything does happen for a reason. Maybe we'll never figure things out.

—Maybe. We don't know how it's all connected. Little things cause big changes.

—Sure, you mean the butterfly effect.

—That has a name?

—Yes.

—I'll have to look that up. I like that you've given me all these ideas to read up on.

—Can you read while posing?

—I read or watch videos on my phone, but I have to be careful what I watch.

—Why?

—I can't watch funny stuff, or I might laugh. That would be distracting.

—I get it.

—I like videos of people falling down . . . but not if they get hurt.

—What do you read?

—Romance novels.

—I should have known.

—Do you have something against romance?

—No, just romance novels.

—Why? They're harmless fun.

—Really? I think they create unrealistic expectations.

—Who decides what's unrealistic?

—My friend was about to get married, but his fiancée dumped him because she wanted him to be more romantic like a character in a vampire novel she was reading.

—Yikes, I see your point. Fantasy and reality tend to ruin each other. It's best to keep them apart.

—Apparently, they can create a potentially volatile mixture. Is that all you read?

—I lied. I don't read romance novels. I read graphic novels.

—You confuse me.

—That's nice to hear. Right now I'm reading one called *Gift Ideas for Artists*.

—I like the title. What's it about?

—It's about a disenchanted artist desperately seeking inspiration.

—Is he seeking a muse?

—You could say that.

—Do you like it?

—Not sure. Sometimes it's beautiful and poetic, other times dull and boring.

—The contrast bothers you?

—No, it's just too much like real life.

—That's bad?

—Yes, I already have a real life. I want a *fantasy* life.

—So does he find a muse?

—I don't know yet. I hope not, because looking for a muse is a waste of time. A muse seeks out an artist who is already working. We want to work with people who can get things done. I would rather work with someone who's working. The best ideas come from working. Why should I waste my time with an artist who isn't serious?

—That seems like a practical approach.

—Oh, yeah. You believe you generate your own ideas.

—Yep, I'm funny that way.

—What do you think intuition is?

—Intuition is based on feelings and unconscious thoughts, so I tend to discount it.

—Oh, really? Why can't you trust your intuition?

—Here's an example. When we look into the sky we see the stars revolve around us. Isn't it reasonable to assume we are the center of the universe?

—I guess it does lead us astray at times. Nothing is foolproof.

—Yes, until scientists revealed the truth. Now we know, as we watch the sunset, that Earth is turning away from the sun. It's not going down.

—True.

—Do you think you can blow a wad of paper into a bottle?

—I guess so. Why not?

—Let's try it.

[He pulls out an empty glass soda bottle from his bag and places it on its side on the table. He then tears out a small piece of paper from his notebook and rolls it into a wad about a half inch round. He places the wad into the opening of the bottle and turns the opening toward her.]

—Okay, let's see if you can blow the wad into the bottle.

—That looks easy.

[She leans forward and makes several attempts to blow the wad into the bottle. Every attempt fails. She sits back in her chair with a confused look on her face.]

—It's surprising, isn't it?

—That's really bizarre. Is this some kind of magic trick?

—No, rudimentary physics.

—Seeing is not always believing.

—Not always.

—But isn't intuition how we make important life decisions? You know, like how we have gut feelings about stuff?

—According to neuroscience, much of our processing is unconscious. You can call that intuition if you want.

—That's interesting.

—May I inquire more about your job?

—Yes, please. I need a break from all this science.

[He laughs.]

—Speaking of free will, do you pick the pose?

—Of course. The model always chooses the pose. I try to pick something creative and sustainable. It's important to look natural and relaxed. If it's forced, it just won't look right.

—So there are no guidelines or parameters? You just make it up?

—I use my intuition. Does that mean it's made up?

—Ha! Very funny.

—I try to do interesting things. I like action poses, so I think in terms of triangles. Diagonals are dynamic. I also practice yoga, so that influences my choices. Sometimes the artists or teachers make suggestions, which makes it collaborative.

—You don't ever just sit there?

—No, sitting or reclining poses bore the artists and me. There's no challenge.

—I can see that.

—Would you like me to demonstrate some poses?

—No, no. That would be inappropriate.

—Inappropriate? So, you're one of those.

—One of what?

—People who are afraid of what others think. See how you're programmed?

—As social animals, conformity is in our genes.

—We are not bound by our genes.

—I guess we'll just have to leave that there.

—Good idea.

—How did you find this particular job? Was this an advertised position? No pun intended.

[She laughs.]

—*Position*. That's a good one. Yes, it's a government job. It's required to be advertised. But I heard about it from a friend. She's also an artist model and she told me about it.

—I see. Speaking of positions, pun intended, after a break, how do you resume the same position?

—Good question. I pick a point on the wall and stare at it. Before the first break, the instructor marks my position on the pedestal with tape, which helps me get back into the same pose.

—So you're literally put on a pedestal.

—Ha! Some call it a model stand, but I prefer pedestal. I like being put on a pedestal. No pun intended.

—So, doing nothing. You make your living doing nothing.

—Yes, in a culture that's obsessed with doing, I do nothing.

—I find that fascinating. Do you enjoy your work?

—Love it. No one talks. I love the silence. It reminds me of nothingness.

—I see how it gives you plenty of time to think.

—Yep, I think a lot. Sometimes I have this hyperawareness of my own heartbeat. I wish there was a word for that.

—Oh, yes. You mentioned something about being superconscious.

—Yep, but sometimes that gets to be too much, so I write dirty limericks in my head. They're hilarious. Wanna hear one?

—No, please. Thank you.

—Oh, yeah. You're shy.

—You can call it that.

—Mostly I think about how frustrating it is to only have one body at a time.

—You mean you want more than one body?

—Yes, don't you?

—No, I'm overwhelmed with having just one.

[She laughs.]

—You're not alone. It seems most people are overwhelmed.

—Have you heard of multiverses?

—Multiverses? No, what's that? Like multiple universes?

—Exactly. It's a theory that postulates that all possibilities in a given situation get played out in its own separate, individual universe. So theoretically there are potentially an infinite number of versions of you in parallel universes.

—That's crazy. I love it.

—Some versions of you will be doing the same thing you're doing now, while others will be wearing a different outfit from your wardrobe, have different careers, different hobbies, or perhaps different personalities. It's infinite.

—Ha! So all the choices I don't make get played out in different worlds?

—Something like that.

—I'll have to look that up. Multiverses.

—That should keep you busy for a while.

—Infinite possibilities. I like that.

—Yes.

—When you look at the night sky you see infinite possibilities, don't you?

—I've never thought of it that way, but I would say that's true. Most people just see specks of lights. They don't think about what they are really seeing.

—I like that about you. Infinity can be scary.

—You mean because they can't fathom it?

—Yes, infinity is a scary thing for lots of people. Terrifying.

—You just take it one star at a time. Star by star.

—One star at a time. I like that. Our sense of wonder and curiosity are really the only things we have going for us.

—You mean as a species?

—Yes.

—I enjoy my opposable thumbs too.

—True, I'll give you that.

—What do you think about when you look up at the stars?

—I want to pluck them out of the sky and eat them.

—That makes no sense.

—It does to me, because I'm always hungry.

—*Ad astra.*

—What's that mean?

—It's Latin for *to the stars.* You've never heard of that?

—I don't speak Latin. Nobody speaks Latin.

—I'm surprised. It's part of many government and college mottoes.

—Interesting.

—The Kansas state motto is *Ad Astra per Aspera.*

—Meaning?

—*Through hardships to the stars.*

—I like that. It makes me want my own motto.

—You should study Latin. It's interesting to see how languages evolve over time.

—I'd like to create my own language.

—Are you dissatisfied with English?

—Yes. There are no words for the really good stuff.

—I see.

—We're taught how to speak, but the words we are using are someone else's words. You know? Not our words. Wouldn't it be great if we could have our own individual language to express ourselves?

—No, if we each had our own individual language, then there would be no communication. No one would be able to understand each other.

—I didn't think about that. I'd have to teach everybody else my language. That seems like a lot of work.

—We are born into a world full of preexisting knowledge. We don't have to discover evolution, algebra, genetics, et cetera. It was already here waiting for us. Language makes that transmission of information possible.

—I guess so. So you speak Latin?

—It's the language of science.

—Isn't that a dead language?

—Not in science.

—Of course, science is your religion.

—It's not a faith.

—Are you sure? You seem to have a lot of faith in the scientific method.

—On the contrary, religion is about faith. Science questions everything.

—Even science itself?

—Yes, science is not dogmatic. It's dynamic. Constantly changing.

—Of course I expect you to defend science. It's your religion.

—You can't believe in science because everything is potentially refutable. Scientists pursue the truth, and we keep one another in check. That's why we can question Einstein.

—The problem is science is limited to what can be observed or measured.

—That's the whole point of science. Galileo said, *Measure what is measurable, and make measurable what is not so.*

—You're missing the point. Science ignores what can't be measured.

—How can we study something that can't be measured?

—Exactly.

—Are you talking about spirituality again?

—I'm always talking about Oneness. I don't separate. You do that.

—But you said you believe in quantum physics.

—So?

—Well, scientists discovered that. You can't just co-opt what you agree with and ignore the rest.

—Why not?

—Because science doesn't exist for your convenience.

—Of course it does. Besides, scientists didn't discover quantum theory.

—No? Then who did?

—The mystic poets of Persia talked about that way before science.

—Oh, really?

—Persian mystical poets talked about quantum physics. Rumi wrote about *dancing atoms*. Aren't you curious what else he had to say?

—Not interested in poetry. Remember? Poetry is too vague.

—I guess you're not that curious about the *truth*.

—I hate to burst your bubble, but Rumi didn't invent atomic theory, it was already around. Democritus developed the classical theory of atomism around 400 BC.

—Was he a poet?

—No, he was a Greek philosopher.

—I bet he was a poet.

—He was a philosopher. Look it up.

—I'll have to look that up.

—The word *atom* comes from the Greek word *atomos*, meaning *indivisible*.

—I'll stick to questions of values.

—Did it ever occur to you that you underappreciate science?

—Did it ever occur to you that you underappreciate nonsense?

—Particle physics may have been the domain of poets and philosophers in the past, but now it belongs to scientists.

—Humans created art and poetry before science, so maybe they are more important.

—Art is a luxury.

—Space exploration is a luxury.

—Are you saying my life's work is a waste of time?

—No, you said that.

—What's your point then?

—You could be doing more to end human suffering.

—Human suffering is the result of religious persecution, political conflicts, oppression, racism, et cetera. These are value-based questions. Science can't help with that.

—You mentioned that before.

—Well, you seem upset, so I guess I'll get back to my work. [He picks up his thesis.]

—Spencer. Spencer. Spencer. Talk to me.

[He ignores her for a few seconds.]

—Wait. How do you know my name?

—It's right there on the cover of your thesis thingy. It's on your coffee cup too.

—Oh, I forgot I put the cover on. Oh, yeah, the cup.

—I'm worried about all this negative energy in the air.

—I'm not concerned about negative energy.

—Why not?

—Because it doesn't exist.

—Of course it does.

—Do you worry about going to hell?

—No.

—Why not?

—Because it doesn't exist.

—I rest my case.

—Well, I have to do something about it. I can't be around negative energy.

—Ha! What are you going to do?

—Discharge it.

—What is the protocol for discharging negative energy?

—Well, since I know your name, would you like to know mine?

—Sure, why not?

—My name is Nancy Esting.

—Esting? What kind of name is Esting? German?

—I don't know. It's made up.

—Made up? You made up your own name? Can you do that?

—Of course. Anyone can. It's a free country.

—So you chose a random name and adopted it?

—Yes. You make me sound so reckless. I tested the name first, of course.

—Tell me about your rigorous name-testing protocol.

—I went to a coffee joint and ordered a coffee with the name Nancy. It felt natural. Nothing weird about it, so I figured it was okay.

—That's it?

—That's all I needed.

—Did you change it legally?

—No, I try to avoid legal stuff and government things.

—I see. So what's your birth name?

—I don't remember. Oh, wait, I think I have an old driver's license with that name.

[She pulls it from her phone wallet and hands it to him. He inspects it closely.]

—Nasreen Noor? Is that an Iranian name?

—Yes! How did you know?

—I have Iranian colleagues. I've picked up a few words from them. Your interest in Persian mystics now makes sense.

—My dad is from Iran, and Mom is American. I'm an L.A. child. My mom is half Black and a million other things. Cherokee. German. Irish.

—So you're mixed race.

—I prefer the term *hybrid*. I'm a hybrid human.

[He looks closely at the license again.]

—This doesn't even look like you, and it's expired.

—Maybe you're right. Maybe it's not me. It's hard to know these days.

—You don't drive?

—Nope, I take the bus or walk.

—Does *Nancy Esting* have some kind of origin story?

—I'm glad you asked. I was walking down the street, and I saw a neon sign in a window that said FREE NANCY ESTING. I wondered who Nancy Esting was, so I walked over to check it out. When I got closer I realized that part of the sign was burned out, and it was supposed to say FREE PREGNANCY TESTING. It turns out it was a women's health center.

—And why were you inspired to take that as a name?

—I was thinking about changing my name and this was a sign. No pun intended.

—Like an omen?

—Exactly. *Esting* is good because it's half of *interesting*. It's also very close to *eating*. I like eating. It's really quite perfect. Divine intervention.

—So the universe speaks to you through broken signs?

—Sometimes. Not always.

—What are the other ways?

—Sometimes strangers on the street tell me things, especially when I'm waiting for the bus.

—Such as?

—One time a man on the street yelled at me, *I'm not homeless. I'm home-free.*

—Was he implying having a home is a burden?

—Exactly. I love that. So profound.

—If you say so.

—How does the universe speak to you?

—Through math equations.

—Ha! Very funny.

—Do you have a business card with your name on it? Or a utility bill?

—Why? Don't you believe that's my name?

—Not really. That's quite a story. It wouldn't be the first time you lied.

—If I were lying, I would have told you by now.

—I don't know what to believe. You don't exactly have any credibility at this point.

—None? Wow, I guess I'll have to work on that.

—Not likely. You don't care about credibility.

—That's not entirely true.

—Only partially true? Then why don't you have a business card?

—Because I'm not a salesperson. I'm not trying to sell anything. Do you have a card?

[He pulls out his wallet and hands her a card.]

—*Spencer Sucher*. That's a good name. You don't need to change it.

[She flips it over, writes something on the back, and hands it back to him.]

—Writing your name on my card is not evidence of truth, Nancy Esting.

—What do you know about the truth?

—I'm a scientist. My life is devoted to seeking the truth.

—Hardly, your life is devoted to impressing your bosses. You're not a revolutionary, you're a conformist.

—No, I'm a skeptic. I question everything. How could I be a conformist?

—If you were truly a skeptic, you'd be skeptical of your own skepticism.

—Skeptical of my own skepticism? Interesting.

—Something you forget to consider.

—Maybe. I'm not sure what that means, but it sounds like something that warrants further investigation.

—See? It means something that doesn't need questioning.

—That sounds like faith.

—Conformity is always a danger.

—We're social animals, so we need to be taught how to function in a society.

—We're programmed to be followers! That robs us of our individuality.

—We're also taught to stop at red lights. Do you find that objectionable?

—What does a yellow light mean? Speed up or slow down?

—What makes you an expert on truth seeking?

—My life is devoted to truth seeking. I'm a mystic.

—What does *mystic* mean to you?

—A mystic is someone who's interested in the interconnectedness of all things. The basic tenets of mysticism are that everything is connected and constantly changing. I don't feel like the world is just a collection of objects. Everything is related somehow in some holistic way.

—Like I said, I can relate to that.

—Do you feel connected to all things?

—Not sure. But I'm not a mystic.

—We are not separate. That's an illusion. We are connected to each other and everything. Those who want power divide us from each other and ourselves.

—Like religions?

—God has been used against us.

—So, you're a theist?

—When I say *God* I mean the great universal life force. It's in all of us.

—I see. So, not the bearded guy in heaven?

—I told you I don't believe in hell, so I guess I can't believe in heaven either.

—Jails aren't filled with atheists, so I don't think we need religion for anything.

—So your parents never made you go to church?

—My mom did, but my dad is an atheist. He believes religion is a tool for mind control.

—My mom made my dad and me go to church with her. When they passed the collection basket, my dad would put in a five-dollar bill and take out a twenty. He was resentful.

—Wow, that's really subversive.

—Sometimes he couldn't sit through the sermon, so he'd read the newspaper in the car.

—I don't blame him. The Church has a long history of persecuting scientists going back to Galileo.

—Oh, yeah. The Church believed Earth was the center of the universe . . . Don't you look around and wonder how everything got here?

—That's pretty much all I do.

—So where did all this come from then? The big bang?

—Perhaps. But what caused the big bang?

—Good question.

—Perhaps the big bang created God.

—Maybe. I like that. Then why don't you believe in God or something?

—What's God have to do with that?

—Because, you goof, God created everything.

—So, now you're an authority on intelligent design?

—Seriously, why don't you believe in God? Because of your parents?

—You believe in God because it's a simple universal explanation. But for me it doesn't answer anything. If I believed God created everything, then I need to ask what created God.

—Is that why so many scientists are atheists?

—I'm not sure most scientists are atheists, but I know that historically religion has not been kind to scientists.

—Yeah, but there's no proof God doesn't exist.

—You're right. That's why I'm not an atheist. I'm agnostic.

—So, what do you think happens when we die?

—We turn back into dust.

—Just like that? We have no souls?

—I don't know. I don't have any way to investigate the matter.

—So you're just a piece of meat?

—Sure, I can live with that.

—Wow, you really don't care about this stuff.

—Do you think trees and dolphins sit around thinking about God?

—I like that image. I need to hold on to it for a second.

—If they don't, then why should I?

—Maybe they do.

—Okay, another impasse. Now that introductions have been made, I'll just get back to my work.

[He picks up his thesis.]

—Do you think this thesis will make you famous?

[He puts the thesis back down.]

—Not likely. It's pretty esoteric.

—Do you want to be famous?

—Only to the extent it facilitates my work.

—Good answer. Fame is overrated.

—I don't understand the obsession with fame. Why reward narcissistic behavior?

—Yep, everybody wants to be special. I hate that.

—We all have egos.

—You know what else I hate?

—What?

—I hate metaphors.

—Why? What did they do to you?

—People use them to elevate things, to make experiences more special than they are. I want to accept everything for what it is. Some things don't have meaning.

—You mean like being famous?

—Exactly.

—Is sitting here with me a meaningful experience?

—No, I wanted to sit at that table because I wanted a window seat. But that guy denied me.

[She points to me, and I casually look away again. I get the sense that she knows I'm watching her and doesn't care. Maybe she likes it. Maybe she's an exhibitionist. Or a narcissist.]

—So, you're not happy about sitting here with me?

—There is no good or bad. That's just a preference that we overlay on top of our experiences. But it's been *interesting* chatting with you.

—*Amor fati.*

—Sounds like you're speaking Latin again. What's it mean?

—Never heard that? It's Latin for *love of fate*.

—I should love my fate?

—It refers to an outlook on life where one attempts to see life events as positive even if they involve suffering.

—I don't feel obligated to love anything. I try to be neutral when I can, but I still have feelings about things that I can't deny. Sometimes I hate things, and that's okay.

—Suit yourself. How about you? Do you want to be famous?

—I'd like to be famous for being anonymous.

—That makes no sense.

—There are lots of paintings that feature artist models we know nothing about. Do we know anything about Mona Lisa?

—I see. We know little about the models in those paintings.

—We all want to be special, but we're not. We want it because we think it'll bring us more love, but it just creates more separation. Separation is the opposite of love.

—How do you propose we get closer to others then?

—By not trying to be special.

—By being ordinary then?

—Yes, that eliminates the barriers to love.

—Does that make sense?

—Why must you always be trying to make sense of things? That seems like a terrible way to live. How do you ever expect to figure this all out?

—I'm not trying to figure out *everything*.

—Are you sure? It seems to me like you are.

—I'm trying to create more questions.

—Questions are good.

—I think the mysteries we are left with can be solved by asking the right questions. If I can solve just a couple of major riddles, I can die happy. We don't know what we are capable of until we try.

—Maybe. So you think everything can be solved?

—I wouldn't be a good scientist if I thought otherwise.

—I guess not.

—So what are some *good* questions?

—You mean what else do I think about?

—Sure.

—The human condition.

—What about it?

—The difference between my fears and my desires. Is dissatisfaction the human condition? Is everyone always frustrated and sad? If so, how can I be more welcoming to the sadness? Or drive it away? I want to be at peace with everything that happens.

—That seems like a tall order.

—Do you have emotional issues?

—Not that I'm aware of.

—Why do we contemplate our sadness but not our happiness?

—I hope that's a rhetorical question.

—No, I'd really like an answer.

—Are you happy?

—I'm not trying to be happy. I'm trying to live an interesting life.

—How's that working out for you?

—Very well, thank you. I think everything should be designed to produce interesting experiences. Not just museums but hospitals too. And schools!

—You want to prioritize having interesting experiences over everything else?

—Sure, why not?

—What's wrong with the pursuit of happiness? That's in the Declaration of Independence.

—Seeking happiness causes misery.

—Huh?

—If you're trying to be happy, then you must constantly monitor yourself to see if you're happy or not. That's what causes unhappiness.

—That's an interesting perspective.

—Also, happiness usually involves achieving some kind of security. Security means avoiding change. And we all know change is inevitable, so security means struggling against reality.

—I like your rhetoric, but I don't spend any time thinking about happiness.

—Maybe there's too much math in there.

—Ha! That might be true.

—I need to think about stuff like this or all I'll be doing is writing dirty limericks.

—I can see in your line of work you'd need things to keep your mind occupied.

—Speaking of which, why do you think we're here?

—I haven't put much thought into that. I mean, not like you have.

—It's all just an experiment. I would think as a scientist you'd know that. We are here to experiment over and over again, until we figure out something that sticks.

—You mean right and wrong?

—I don't believe in dichotomies like right and wrong. Or good and evil.

—That sounds vague.

—That's because it is. There's no magic formula. It's about ending suffering.

—Now we're getting into values again.

—You're right. We can't be objective. We are emotional animals.

—That's what neuroscience tells us.

—We're not machines. They can't feel, think, or create.

—Well actually, artificial intelligence can create all kinds of things.

—Sure, after the machines are trained by humans.

—That's true.

—Ask me another.

—Hmm . . . if you weren't a muse, what would you be doing?

—Easy. I'd be panning for gold in Alaska. Next question.

—Really? People still do that?

—A friend of mine is up there, and she sends me a tiny vial of gold dust every year for my birthday.

—Did you have another job before beginning your modeling career?

—I worked at a copy store. It was a national chain. I was fired. Can I tell you that story?

—What was the reason for your termination?

—Oh, you'll like this. I was fired for being too empathetic.

—Empathetic? That's an undesirable quality in the copy world?

—Apparently. You see, sad kids would come in and want flyers made for lost pets. You know, like the ones you see on telephone poles. Heartbreaking.

—Sure. Those flyers always make me sad.

—Well, they were just kids, so they never had enough money. They were so sad. I would make the copies and not charge them. I figured no one would notice. Well, one day there was a scary lightning storm and lots of pets ran away. I made lots of free copies that week.

—So your manager noticed?

—Yep, I was fired for *failing to optimize strategic and tactical initiatives*.

—What does that mean?

—It doesn't mean anything! It's corporate nonsense!

—That doesn't sound like a good place for you.

—Needless to say I didn't thrive there. Would you like to hear a sample performance review?

—Sure, if you must.

—*According to our metrics, you're not being multifunctional and collaborative in your approach to expediting strategic best practices.*

—Why do you have that memorized?

—To remind me what assholes they are.

—They seem fond of the word *strategic.*

—I know! What's that about? It's so uncreative and oppressive.

—Corporations thrive on predictability.

—True. Our economy thrives on insecurity and dissatisfaction.

—Sure, advertisers exploit that.

—Corporations don't care about my hopes and dreams. They just want me to buy stuff.

—That's their job.

—My manager liked to say it was his job to make things manageable.

—Is that a pun?

—I don't think so. What do you think?

—Not sure, that's why I asked.

—At least my parents were proud.

—Proud of your corporate thievery?

—No, silly. They liked that I helped the kids. I wish I could still help them, but we can't save everyone, right?

—Sad but true. I often think about that in the context of searching for exoplanets.

—Oh, right. You're looking for other planets that humans can live on.

—I have mixed feelings. Sometimes I want to save the world. Other times I'm consumed by the sheer futility of it all. The endgame is Earth will stop spinning and collide with the sun. Or get pummeled by asteroids. Or the sun will fizzle out and implode. Have you considered that?

—No, but I will now. Thanks for that.

—Everything has an endgame. Cycle of life.

—I don't like thinking about it because it's too depressing.

—Well, then religion should appeal to you. It provides solace and the illusion of permanence in an ever-changing world.

—Religion is stagnation.

—Yes, that's precisely its appeal.

—I don't need false comfort. Or real comfort.

—There's hope for you.

—I have a problem with prayer too.

—That's seems like the most benign part of it.

—Oh, no. That's duality. If you believe in Oneness, then you can't pray. If you're part of the integral whole of everything, then who are you praying to? Yourself?

—That's an interesting perspective. Prayer seems like begging to me.

—What do you think is going to happen when you're gone?

—You mean dead? Didn't you already ask me that? I don't know.

—Yeah.

—I have no clue where I came from, so why would I know where I'm going?

—You spend all your time thinking about life but no time thinking about death.

—Odd but true.

—It does seem odd.

—I've never been interested in metaphysics or spirituality.

—Not interested? Most are consumed by a fear of death.

—Yes, mortality seems to be a pressing issue for many, but I have more pressing issues to consider.

—Life on other planets?

—Mainly. And you?

—Heaven sounds nice, but the price of admission seems rather high.

—Not worth it?

—I'm leaning toward reincarnation these days.

—I don't get how there are enough souls to keep recycling them.

—Huh?

—If there are more people alive now than have ever lived, then don't we need new souls?

—Oh, well, you're forgetting about life on other planets and in other dimensions.

—Of course. Silly me, I forgot about the aliens.

—That's surprising coming from a man who's studying Martians.

[She taps his thesis.]

—Once again, I study the Martian atmosphere, not Martians. But as a fan of Carl Sagan, I'm aware of the possibilities. Like I said.

—Speaking of aliens, what do you know about that face on Mars that aliens built?

—Are you referring to the one on the Cydonian mesa?

—Huh? How many faces are there on Mars?

—I've seen a few. Seeing faces is a common form of pareidolia. Neurological evidence suggests that our facial-processing mechanisms can be fooled into seeing humanoid faces in random stimuli. The man in the moon is another example.

—No, the one I saw was real. NASA released a photo of it.

—Did you see the high-resolution photos from the Mars Global Surveyor? When you see it from other perspectives it looks similar to the land formations around it. I assure you it was an optical illusion, not the work of extraterrestrials.

—Maybe it's a conspiracy? Maybe NASA is hiding evidence of aliens?

—If that were true, why would NASA release the photos in the first place?

—Wait, you're right. That makes no sense. They could've just kept it to themselves.

—Right.

—I'm going to ask my dad about that. He's a conspiracy nut.

—Before you discuss it with him, look at the photos of the Galle Crater.

—Why?

—It has a smiley face.

—I'll have to look that up.

—Speaking of your dad, what does he think of your *nude* modeling?

—Are you afraid of what your parents think?

—No, just curious.

—My dad is supportive, but my mom's against it. He's got flexible boundaries, so I can't take his support seriously.

—I'm confused.

—So am I. He was in prison a few times for art fraud. He says he was framed. No pun intended.

—Is that like art forgery?

—Exactly. When he was a young struggling artist he resented successful artists, so he forged their art. It wasn't his idea. He was tricked into it. I'm not sure what the details are. He considered himself to be an unrecognized genius.

—Did he ever find success?

—Ironically, he's a successful artist now because of the fame he achieved as an art forger.

—He doesn't sound like much of a moral authority.

—Ha! That didn't stop him from calling me from prison to discipline me.

—How did he discipline you from prison?

—Well, when he called from prison my mom would complain about me, and then when I got on the phone he'd lecture me and tell me to stand in the corner.

—I still can't understand how someone in prison can have any moral authority.

—It's not *moral* authority. It's *paternal* authority. I listened to him because he was my dad. He was really concerned I'd end up a thief like him.

—He didn't exactly lead by example.

—No, but I learned a lot from his negative example.

—Have you ever been arrested?

—No.

—Then I guess it worked.

—Ha! I guess so.

—Is he out now?

—He's on probation or something. Not sure.

—You don't know?

—He's not exactly transparent. He's always working in his studio. He never leaves. He could have an ankle monitor and no one would know.

—I'm afraid to ask, but what kind of work does he produce?

—Dark abstracts.

—Dark colors?

—Dark colors and dark imagery.

—I see.

—Yep, he's a painter who's inspired by his dark past.

—Dark past? What happened to him?

—I don't know. He won't talk about it.

—He sounds disturbed.

—Well-adjusted people don't become artists.

—If you say so. Well, at least he has met with some success.

—Maybe too much success.

—How so?

—He owes a lot of money to the IRS. He's against paying taxes. They stop by his studio regularly to try to seize any work he produces.

—Sounds like he has some serious authority issues.

—Sure does. He figured out a clever hack. Now he paints on the wall so the IRS can't seize the paintings. You know, because the wall's part of the building.

—But doesn't that prevent him from selling them too?

—Ha! No! When the paintings are finished he calls his collectors over. They pick the ones they like, and he then cuts them out of the wall.

—Interesting. Devious but clever.

—That's my dad in a nutshell.

—You're the most transparent person I've ever met.

—Really? Do you like it?

—I don't think so.

—Some people tell me it's refreshing.

—On the contrary, I find it alarming.

—Alarming? Why?

—I don't know. I guess because it's not normal.

—Oh, I see. You must have secrets you want to hide.

—Maybe. I think most people would make an effort to hide family criminal histories.

—Oh, your father got arrested too?

—I didn't say that.

—You didn't have to. Communication is mostly non-verbal. Spill it.

—There's nothing to talk about.

—If you don't tell me what your dad did, I'll assume it's something really bad like murder.

—No, no, nothing like that.

—So he *was* arrested.

—It was a drug charge. He experimented with marijuana when he was a kid and got caught.

—No jail time?

—No charges were filed.

—You're embarrassed by that? That's nothing.

—I'm only embarrassed because he is. He's a prominent doctor. I shouldn't be talking about this.

—My dad thinks he's Thoreau. Getting arrested is a form of activism. Protest.

—Wasn't Thoreau protesting slavery?

—Yes. My dad's noble cause is himself.

—Sounds like it.

—Ask me more questions.

—A change of subject would be a good idea.

—Ask me anything. I'm transparent!

—Okay, what are your challenges in modeling?

—Boredom mostly. Coffee helps, but then I have to pee. I need distractions.

—Distractions?

—Yeah, when I'm not reading or on my phone I work on my novel.

—You mean in your head?

—Yeah, in my head. Where else?

—I see. I'm afraid I'm not familiar with the creative writing process. What's your novel about?

—It's about a flower who wants to be human who meets a human that wants to be a flower.

—I don't know what that means.

—It's semiautobiographical.

—Huh? Semiautobiographical?

—Yep, they say all fiction is autobiographical.

—Are you the flower or the human?

—Both. I'm the flower *and* the human. It's about Oneness, the interconnectedness of all things. You know, it's about those feelings.

—You mean feelings in general?

—Exactly. How can we know if what we are feeling is real? When something bad happens, how do we know how long we should grieve? Should we spend our lives trying to be happy? Do we love our loved ones enough? Should we question our feelings or just accept them?

—Sounds ambitious and perhaps torturous. Why torment yourself with writing such a novel?

—I have novelist friends, and I feel left out when they talk about writing.

—You're writing a novel just so you have something to talk about?

—Basically.

—Is that a good reason to write a novel?

—I'm not sure there is a good reason to write a novel.

—I'm confused.

—Why? You're doing the same thing.

—I am? How so?

—Aren't you writing your thesis thingy so you can have something to talk about?

—That's a gross oversimplification, but I'm afraid it might be true.

—Why torment yourself with writing such an ambitious and torturous thesis?

—Ha! You're quite the wit.

—There's no good reason to write a novel.

—I see. So . . . how far along are you?

—I'd rather not say. It's bad luck to talk about it. I'm superstitious.

—I didn't mean to pry. I'm not familiar with the proper protocol regarding inquiring about creative projects.

—I only have the first line.

—What is it?

—*I don't get lonely, so I forget others do.*

—Sounds like a good start, but it seems you have some work ahead of you.

—Ha. Maybe. But maybe the point is to not finish it. Not everything can be written, you know? Not everything can be healed by talking. Maybe talking makes you worse off.

—Are you suggesting you don't intend to complete it?

—There are too many distractions in life: friends, coffee, and delicious baked goods.

—This is true. It takes discipline.

—A couple years ago, I decided to focus my life on it, so I tricked my friends into thinking I moved to Manhattan. You know, so I could be alone and work without interruptions. I had a going-away party and everything. I had moving boxes around the apartment as props.

—Wait, you faked moving away?

—Yep, I got a voice mail box and a mailing address in New York and everything.

—It seems like you put a lot of thought and effort into this elaborate hoax. Did it work?

—For a while, but eventually they found out. Apparently, someone saw me at the supermarket and told everyone. They were really mad.

—I can understand that. I don't blame them for being mad.

—Why are you taking their side?

—I'm not taking sides. I don't even know these people. I don't even know you!

—I'm kidding. It was dumb. I apologized. We're all good now.

—That's good to hear.

—Yep, it's good.

—Good, I'm glad. It's hard to believe a novel would be that important to you. More important than your friends.

—The idea of being able to transfer my thoughts into another person's mind is appealing to me. What about you? Are there any conversations in your book?

—There's no dialogue in a thesis. It's not a work of fiction.

—Sounds boring. Your readers would enjoy it more if it were more entertaining.

—It's not supposed to be entertaining.

—Then I have no plans to read it.

—That's okay. I didn't write it for you, so I don't really care.

—What *do* you care about then?

—I don't understand the question.

—Okay, then what do you do for fun?

—Why are you asking so many questions?

—It's not personal. I want to know about everyone.

—Are you implying the study of the Martian atmosphere is not fun?

—But that's work. I'm talking about hobbies or interests. What do you think about when you're not thinking about Mars?

—You really want to know?

—Of course. I'm being sincere.

—My sister.

—That's sweet. Are you worried about her? Is she ill?

—No, nothing like that. She's fine.

—Well then?

—I'd like your insight into something.

—What is it? Is it something about your sister?

—Yes. It's hard to explain . . . I guess . . . I want to be like her.

—More feminine?

—No!

—What then?

—I don't know . . . what is it . . . I guess I would have to say *outgoing*.

—Like friendly?

—Perhaps *friendly* is a better word.

—Why do you want to be friendly?

—I'd like to be better at small talk. You know, a better conversationalist. She's good at that. She can walk into a party and strangers instantly become friends.

—And how does she do that?

—I have no idea. That's why I'm asking you. You obviously have no problem talking to strangers.

—That's true. Can you give an example? Paint a picture for me. Pun intended.

—She walks into a party and walks up to someone. It seems to start with a compliment, like *I love your earrings*. Then they say, *Oh, my boyfriend gave them to me for Valentine's Day*. Then they start talking about boyfriends. Or *I like your sweater* turns into a discussion about shopping, and next thing you know they are the best of friends.

—Have you tried the same technique?

—Yes, but my compliments don't seem to have the same effect. Sometimes they get interpreted as insults. My sister has even tried to coach me. But she says I'm hopeless. Are you familiar with this technique?

—Of course. I can do that, but I choose not to.

—Why? You don't want to be friendly?

—Small talk is boring. I prefer inappropriate personal questions. I like to break things open so I can see what's inside. I like to turn over rocks by the river to see what's underneath.

—I noticed.

—I only talk to interesting people.

—Does that mean I'm interesting?

—Of course.

—Because I'm a scientist?

—No, because you're awkward.

—Ah, yes. I remember you like awkwardness. I'm having a hard time figuring you out.

—What's there to figure out? Maybe that's your problem. People don't want to be analyzed. They want to be accepted for who they are.

—I guess. I'm not sure what to do about that.

—Calm down. Just be yourself.

—That's a meaningless cliché.

—Clichés become clichés because they contain bits of truth. That's why they get passed on.

—Don't you think this conversation is awkward?

—Yes, that's why I like it. You're being you and I'm being me. It's authentic.

—Why do I feel so uncomfortable then?

—Because you're struggling against reality.

—Isn't that how we improve?

—Practice can improve skills but can't change one's nature.

—You're suggesting that I embrace my awkwardness?

—An awkward conversation is better than none at all.

—Because it's authentic?

—Yep, this is real life. You know what normal people do?

—I have no idea.

—Small talk!

—Small talk is bad?

—Of course. Isn't it obvious?

—So discussing the weather is bad?

—Small talk is an attempt to connect without emotional risk.

—I never thought of it that way.

—No risk, no gain. Don't try to be someone else. Be who you are.

—I'm giving this careful consideration.

—If someone tries to change you, it means they have an agenda.

—That makes sense. I appreciate all this. You're smart.

—What's that supposed to mean?

—I'm just saying you're smart. It's a compliment.

—You mean smart for an artist model?

—Are you upset?

—Did you expect me to be dumb based on my appearance and profession?

—No, no . . . I . . . I didn't know what to expect . . . at first.

—And now?

—I still don't know what to expect.

—I'm kidding. I was just messing with you.

—Don't do that!

—You're like a man who injured his leg and started using a cane, and now he relies on the cane even though his leg is healed. As he walks down the street a passerby kicks his cane out of his hand. He stands there cursing until he realizes he doesn't need the cane.

—I'm the man in this metaphor?

—Yes.

—What is the nature of my injury?

—Your education. It limits your worldview.

—I see. So you're saying education is bad.

—Not if it expands your world. I'm just trying to keep you on your toes.

—Well, I think it's mean.

—I wouldn't do it if I didn't think you could handle it.

—That sounds like a compliment.

—That's a huge compliment!

—You're a strange bird.

—I have a confession, since we are being honest.

—What now?

—I lied about everything.

—What do you mean? What else did you lie about?

—There's no novel.

—No novel? So you fabricated the moving story?

—Yes. You seem disappointed.

—I liked you better when you lied.

—It wasn't really a lie. It was a conversation starter.

—More like a conversation ender.

—Maybe if you're lucky I will lie again. Ask me more.

—Why bother?

—It was just an experiment.

—So you're experimenting on me?

—Humans are constantly experimenting on each other.

—I've never thought of it that way. You're probably right.

—Humanity is a giant social experiment. We do and say things to test other people's reactions all the time.

—That seems so disingenuous.

—How else are we supposed to figure out who we are?

—There's got to be a better way.

—There isn't. Ask me more.

—Fine. What do *you* do for fun?

—I listen to music and spin around. The cosmic dance of Shiva, the endless cycle of creation and destruction. I like circular motion. Did you know that's the most common type of motion in the universe?

—Of course. I have a degree in quantum physics, remember?

—Of course. Everything is made of empty space and spinning particles. Everything seems solid but it's just energy. Matter is energy. Isn't that crazy?

—No, it's just plain old reality. Just because we don't have answers now doesn't mean we won't have them in the future.

—I like the mystery.

—I like making discoveries.

—Not everything is a problem to be solved.

—Maybe. Maybe not.

[He picks up his thesis again.]

—Speaking of answers, ask me something.

—Why? It seems rather pointless at this juncture. I need to work.

—Come on! Be a good sport.

—Are you really an artist model?

—Yes.

[He sets his thesis down.]

—This has been very awkward for me. I hope you're happy.

—What's the most awkward situation you've ever been in?

—I'd have to say the one I'm in right now.

—It could be worse.

—How?

—What if we were to have a staring contest?

—Is this another one of your social experiments?

—Yes. You said you wanted honesty.

—Why a staring contest?

—I think it will help your social skills. Are you ready?

—No, I refuse.

—Well, I'm going to start, and you can catch up when you're ready.

—Well, you can't force me.

[He looks out the window to avoid her gaze.]

—You're not even trying. Come on.

[After a minute he looks over at her again and seems to lock eyes with her.]

—Little Dipper?

—What?

—It's the Little Dipper.

—Are you talking about the freckles on my eye?

—Yes, they look like the Little Dipper. In the lower part of your right eye. Seven red dots contrasting against the green of your iris.

[She blushes and covers her face.]

—I'm sorry, did I say something wrong?

—No, it's fine. It's just that no one has ever noticed that before.

—Really? But it's so obvious.

—You're the first person to notice it.

—Are you embarrassed? I'm sorry.

—No, it's okay. I'm not sure what I'm feeling. It's kind of sweet in a creepy kind of way. I wish there were a word to describe it.

—*Creepy* doesn't sound good.

—Sorry, more like exposed.

—Exposed? You're often nude in front of strangers and *now* you feel exposed?

—Odd, isn't it?

—Well, if it's any consolation, I wish I had a star chart on my iris.

—It's pretty cool, but the Pleiades would be better.

—Pleiades? Why?

—Because I'm from there.

—You're an alien? No wonder you keep asking about Martians.

—Don't you think it's curious that only six stars are visible, but somehow the Mayans knew there were seven stars? How did they know that?

—I don't know anything about Mayans or aliens.

[He pulls a magnifying glass out of his bag, holds it up, and leans toward her.]

—May I?

[She shrugs and leans forward so he can examine her retina. She stays remarkably still during this process. I guess that's to be expected of an artist model.]

—Can I see that?

[She grabs the magnifying glass and holds it up to a shaft of sunlight coming through the window. She focuses the sunlight into a bright dot on his arm.]

—Does that hurt?

—Not yet.

—How about now?

[He yanks his arm away with a yelp and rubs the spot.]

—Now it hurts!

—That's just one kind of pain.

—The Little Dipper is good. It has the North Star in it. Polaris.

—I guess I do like the North Star. It's easy to find.

—Definitely. The stars of the Northern Hemisphere appear to rotate around it, so it was an important navigational tool for ancient mariners.

—Yep.

—It appears stationary because it seems to be aligned with Earth's axis, but it's actually off by 0.7 degree.

—You sure know a lot of obscure trivia.

—Trivia? Astronomy is my life.

—Are you interested in astrology too?

—No, why?

—If you were an astrologer, you could put that planetary trivia to good use.

—I'm not interested in divination. I'm interested in science.

—Astrology, astronomy. They're the same to me. Both are interesting.

—Trust me, there's a huge distinction.

—Maybe in the eye of the beholder.

—How can you believe in free will *and* astrology?

—What's the problem?

—Astrology means we're predestined. Our fate is determined by the position of celestial bodies. That means no free will. My understanding is that fate and free will are mutually exclusive.

—It's not like that.

—Well? Are we predestined as astrology says? Or do we have free will? So what is the point of divining your future if you have no free will?

—*It's not like that.* You're not getting it.

—How is it then?

—Don't you have fortune-telling in math and science?

—Fortune-telling in science? No, we don't have that.

—Yeah, it's called data science or something like that.

—Data science makes predictions? Are you talking about predictive analytics?

—Yep, that's it. You said that predicts people's behavior.

—That doesn't really predict the future. It identifies trends.

—There you go. That's what astrology does. It identifies trends.

—So within the framework of astrology we have free will? We have some say in our lives?

—We have free will, but not as much as people think.

—So we just have a little bit of free will?

—Exactly.

—Just enough free will to influence our lives?

—Sure.

—Maybe we choose our career or spouse?

—Sounds about right. You'd be a good astrologer since you know all the technical stuff.

—I'll take that as a compliment, but it'll never happen.

—Do you ever think about the names of the constellations?

—Sure, I have a passing interest in planetary nomenclature.

—So, then you know storytellers named the constellations. Poets and shaman looked into the sky and made up stories. That helped them cope with the mysteries of life. Isn't that where the names of constellations come from?

—Perhaps, but now we have science. New planets are given numbers.

—That's sad.

—Well, you'll be happy to know it's common to name new planetary features after rock bands, cartoon characters, and ice cream. That's our mythology now.

—Really? That sounds fun.

—I believe astronomy began as a way to predict the seasons for agricultural purposes.

—Tell me your birthday.

—Why?

—I want to know your star sign.

—That's nonsense.

—Okay, then I'll guess your sign.

—Please don't.

—You're pretty analytical, so I bet you're an Aquarius, an air sign.

—Let's drop it. Do you really believe there are only twelve kinds of people on Earth?

—Twelve kinds? Oh, you mean because there are twelve signs. Yeah, it's way more complicated than that. There's your sun sign, moon sign, rising sign. Lots of possibilities.

—I'm still not interested.

—Come on. Tell me your birthday.

—Well, you brought up programming. Perhaps you were programmed to believe in astrology.

—I'll tell you what Aquarians are like, and you tell me if any of it sounds familiar.

—Not interested.

—You spend much of your time in your head, maybe even *overthinking* things. You obsessively gather information. You prefer numbers to people. You rarely consult your heart. You tell people the truth even if it's painful. You like to challenge conventions and theorize about new ideas. You tend to be impatient with people who aren't as analytical as you. Sound familiar?

—Perhaps, but you could have deduced all that from our conversation.

—I'm guessing your birthday is toward the end of January.

—Fine, just to end this. It's January 30.

—Yes! Smack dab in the middle of Aquarius. I totally called it.

—Are you happy now?

—You should be more open-minded about this stuff.

—There's no scientific evidence to support the premises of astrology.

—It brings a new story to your life so you can see things from a new perspective.

—I'm satisfied with my current narrative.

—Come on. It's harmless and empowering.

—Harmless? You're telling me my fate is sealed. Predestined. That means I have no free will. No agency! Why bother trying if I'm predestined? I find that disempowering.

—Clearly, you've never heard of astrological magic then.

—So, you're a magician too? I'm not interested in magic of any kind.

—That's unfortunate. Astrological magic can help you reduce problematic issues in your birth chart. You should practice it, because it gives you some power over your fate. Otherwise, you're just a victim of planetary forces.

—Are you serious? Do you really believe the gravitational forces of celestial bodies determine your fate?

—Sure, the moon's gravity moves the ocean, so it must affect us too. After all, we're mostly water. Don't you think?

—Do you know what a confirmation bias is?

—I've heard of that.

—You tend to remember outcomes that are consistent with your predictions and ignore the ones that are inconsistent with your beliefs.

—Anything is possible, I guess.

—That's one of the first things you learn about in science. That's why we focus on empirical evidence and logic.

—That's the problem, not the solution. I think you're missing out on a lot of life.

—I think you live in a fantasy world.

—I live in all worlds, including yours. You only live in your world.

—Well, I like thinking critically. Why would I intentionally abandon that?

—Stories and art offer us a different perspective on life. It's a way of exploring society and ourselves.

—Why?

—To experience catharsis.

—Why?

—Haven't you been driven to tears by a thing of beauty?

—Not that I recall.

—What about by a movie?

—Nope.

—Really? Maybe you are a robot.

—Perhaps.

—All humans I know enjoy stories and art. I don't need to explain why they're important. That's what we're doing right now, sharing stories.

—Not everyone is interested in art or stories. I just think they're frivolous.

—If you're obsessed with solutions and productivity, you'll miss the point of art.

—You have an issue with *productivity*?

—I feel that Americans are too obsessed with productivity.

—What's wrong with productivity?

—Time, efficiency, and measuring stuff get emphasized. Everything else gets ignored.

—And that's a problem?

—Yes, because the best parts of life can't be measured. So what can't be measured gets ignored. Humans are only valued as machines. We've become robots.

—Well, that's a question of values.

—And we know how you feel about questions of value.

—I'll stick to my work.

—Art is food for the soul.

—The soul needs nourishment?

—Your soul will starve to death without it.

—Sounds dangerous—what do you recommend?

—Go to museums, listen to music, read stories, and never stop dancing. Never stop dancing.

—Sounds like escapism, a distraction from boredom or pain.

—Would you say food is a distraction from starving to death?

—Food is a necessity.

—Exactly like art is a necessity. Art asks you to feel something, or question something. Art is a necessity.

—Feelings are overrated.

—How can you say that?

—They're fleeting, so they are insignificant.

—I feel sad for you.

—Why do you say that?

—Fleeting things are the most significant because they'll be gone soon.

—Don't worry. Your sadness is fleeting.

—I'm glad I can enjoy fleeting things. Even if they are sad.

—I'm happy for you, but I'll stick to numbers.

—Do you want to know my sign?

—Of course not.

—I'm a Pisces, a water sign. That's associated with spirituality and creativity. Reality and fantasy are constantly competing for my attention. Isn't that perfect?

—You really need to look up cognitive biases.

—Come on, what's the harm in it?

—I just explained it to you.

—I guess I missed it.

—Let me present it another way. As I mentioned, *predestined* means one has no free will. If there's no free will, you can't hold people accountable for their actions.

—I don't get it.

—Okay, do you believe evil people exist in this world?

—Sure, I guess so.

—You can't believe in fate *and* morality. Fate means you have no free will, and therefore you can't be held accountable for your actions. Do you have free will or not?

—I thought so, but now I'm confused.

—You're not sure what you believe? That's called cognitive dissonance. That's when your beliefs are inconsistent, perhaps even contradictory. How do you reconcile your opposing beliefs?

—I guess I don't need to.

—Why not?

—Because I'm not an Aquarius!

—Not again with the astrology!

—Just because something doesn't make sense to *you* doesn't mean it doesn't make sense. You're not all-knowing, you know.

—Non-sense is non-sense. Have you heard of the Socratic method?

—No. Should I?

—It's a dialogue designed to elicit critical thinking in order to achieve clarity and consistency in our ideas.

—Sounds like a lot of work for nothing. And a conversation killer.

—Perhaps, but if you value clarity and consistency, it's worth the effort.

—I live in a world of infinite possibilities. I thought you did too.

—Some possibilities are infinite, but we're also constrained by certain laws—for example, the laws of physics.

—I'm a Pisces, so I'm not analytical. I'm not disadvantaged in that way.

—Disadvantaged? So you consider a preference for rational analysis a handicap?

—You don't hide it very well.

—Agree to disagree, let's talk about something else. Or perhaps nothing at all.

[He picks up his thesis.]

—Wait. I have something to say about free will.

—Well? What is it?

—I'm not sure.

—Are you just a victim of the universe?

—I don't feel like a victim.

—So everything is random then?

—When you noticed the Little Dipper in my eye, you dismissed it as an odd coincidence, but for me it's an affirmation of the interconnectedness of all things. Oneness. I'm part of something bigger than myself. I find meaning and reassurance in that.

—Once again, I'm happy for you. But I don't need meaning or reassurance.

—Really? I think we all do.

—That says a lot more about you than it does about me.

—Fine. Let's leave that there, and let's get back to being human.

—Being human?

—Yes, I liked it when you talked about your sister. What else do you like about your sister?

—My sister?

—Yes.

—I regret bringing her up.

—It's too late for regrets. It's always too late for regrets.

[He rubs his face and head in a dramatic way.]

—She's funny too. I want to be more like that.

—Funnier? More funny? Which is it? I want to get better at puns. Then I can say *no pun intended* or *pun intended*, whichever is funnier. More funny? I think that would be *amusing*. Pun intended. Get it? I'm a muse.

—Yes, quite.

—I think you're too self-conscious to be funny. I have an idea.

[She jumps up on her chair.]

—What are you doing? Get down.

—Watch this.

[She drops her bathrobe. She stands there facing me in her flesh-toned bodysuit. It's then I see the merkin.

Normally, I would not look in that area, but it is right at my eye level. The only reason I know what a merkin is is because my grandpa liked to talk about the sex workers he frequented in Italy during the war. They wore them to pass for blond to appeal to the American soldiers. I try to turn away, but I'm frozen. I close my eyes, hoping I don't become a part of this story.]

—Please get down! Please!

[His face is red.]

—Why?

—You're making a scene. You're embarrassing me.

—Lighten up. It's funny.

—Please. You're making a scene. We'll get kicked out.

[He quickly reaches for her arm but stops. Instead, he starts packing his things. She jumps down, looking worried, and puts her bathrobe back on before sitting down.]

—I'm so sorry, I didn't mean to upset you. I was trying to amuse you. No pun intended.

—I'll be leaving now. Good day.

—Look around. No one is looking at us.

[He stops packing his things and looks around.]

—Why are you so self-conscious?

—I'm not like you. I don't want to draw attention to myself.

—No one cares. I could just be a figment of your imagination. No one here even noticed. Well, except the man behind you who appears to be studying us.

[I freeze again. Am I being too obvious? I feel like the worst PI in the world, but then I remember I'm not on a case.]

—Talk to me. What's going on in your head?

[He finishes collecting his things and places his backpack on his lap. He sits there motionless, hugging his backpack.]

—Like you said, people don't want to be analyzed.

—Well, you reached for me, and now your things are packed. Some decisions have been made, haven't they?

—Wow, you must be psychic!

—Yes, but that's not relevant right now. I see your face. You're self-conscious.

—Isn't it obvious? I'd prefer not to be embarrassed in public. What if a colleague or professor is here?

—Being friendly requires being tolerant and open-minded.

—I don't appreciate your dismissive attitude. You displayed a pubic wig in public! Who does that?

—Thanks for noticing. I like to keep it handy. I find it adds texture to an otherwise barren area.

—I don't know how to respond to that.

—Say you love coffee and sunshine.

—I love coffee and sunshine.

—It's best not to align yourself with other people's values.

—So I guess you don't care what people think?

—It's limited. I don't want to hurt people. I just want to wake them up.

—Are they sleeping?

—Yes, society puts them to sleep, makes them numb. TV. Drugs. Alcohol.

—I've witnessed that firsthand.

—When I was little I had a guinea pig. I kept it in a cage with sawdust on the bottom. It spent all its time digging in the corner. One day a friend came over to see the guinea pig. She told me the guinea pig wanted a house, so I bought a plastic hollow log and put it inside the cage. It crawled inside and never dug again.

—Sure, it's prey, so it wants to be covered.

—Right, I just thought it liked digging, but it was just trying to hide.

—I'm assuming there's a point to this story?

—Some people like to hide, and some like to hide in crowds.

—I get your point. I'm not good at this stuff.

—Don't be so hard on yourself. No one has ever been you before. No one knows how to be you, not even you.

—Perhaps.

—I tried to be friendly.

—Yeah?

—I was like you once. I wanted to have more friends.

—So you can relate?

—Of course.

—What happened?

—You'll like this story because it has math in it.

—Math? I like math.

—I was at a friend's birthday party. This was years ago. There were lots of guests there, like around fifty. It was a fun party, and I thought it would be nice to have a bunch of friends over for a big birthday party. You know, to feel all that love.

—Sounds nice. What happened?

—I did the math and decided against it.

—What's the math?

—I thought the math would be obvious to you. Aren't you a math wiz?

—This doesn't sound like a math problem.

—Okay, here's the math. Try to keep up. In order to have fifty people at your birthday party, you'd be obligated to go to their birthday parties too, right?

—Sounds appropriate.

—So, if you have fifty parties a year to go to, that's like almost one *every* weekend. That means I would be going to birthday parties *every* weekend.

—That's the math part?

—Yes. That's way too many parties for me, so I decided against it.

—That makes sense. That's a lot of parties.

—But I do get lonely sometimes. Not often. Do you?

—Not that I'm aware of. Why is it a problem for you?

—Loneliness? It's hard to explain. Sometimes it's like a craving to be with others.

—I can't relate.

—Aren't you human?

—Last time I checked.

—I'm beginning to think *you're* an alien. That's why you avoid the subject.

—Nonsense, I'm not an alien.

—Do you know the difference between solitude and loneliness?

—Never thought about it. Do you?

—Yes, but I can't explain it.

—I understand we're social animals, so we're hardwired to live in groups. In the past it was critical for our survival.

—It still is.

—Perhaps.

—I guess *solitude* is being alone without feeling lonely.

—Well, biologically speaking, I guess it makes sense to reward socializing behavior with a dopamine response. In contrast, isolation would produce an unpleasant emotional response.

—Yes, like you said, we are social animals.

—I like being alone. I get more work done. It seems to be a subjective experience.

—Subjective? Aren't all feelings subjective?

—Some say they can still feel lonely in the presence of others.

—Yeah, I guess that's true. I've felt that. That's an odd kind of separation.

—The word *alienation* comes to mind.

—Now you brought up *aliens*. Since you brought it up . . .

—Fine. I give up. Let's talk about aliens.

—Really? Because I have a lot of questions.

—You mentioned before that you're an alien from the Pleiades, so you should know more about this subject than I do.

—We're all aliens!

—What are you talking about?

—All the ancients have stories about aliens. Many believed they were descended from beings from the Pleiades. They called their ancestors *sky people* or *star people*.

—Is there any evidence to support this?

—What about all those ancient rock carvings showing those figures with space helmets? Or those giant drawings in South America that can only be seen from space?

—You mean the Nazca Lines in Peru?

—Yeah, that sounds right. One of them looks like an astronaut!

—I would hardly consider that *evidence* of extraterrestrials.

—You don't know what you're talking about. Some space expert you are!

—The ancients believed all kinds of questionable things that I find absurd. The list is long.

—Have you heard of a *vimāna*?

—No.

—They're spaceships in the Vedas, the ancient Hindu scriptures. Those are how the gods got around.

—Gods need transportation?

—I guess so, because they're in the Vedas.

—Why can't these gods just warp the fabric of space-time?

—Not sure. It doesn't get into that sort of stuff.

—Well, do they at least explain how these holy spaceships are powered?

—No! It's not about physics.

—Do they at least mention the fuel source for these spaceships?

—No! You're missing the point.

—So where are the extraterrestrials now?

—We're all mixed together now.

—Mixed together? You mean we all have extraterrestrial DNA?

—Yes! I would think as an astrobiologist you'd take this more seriously.

—We already discussed panspermia.

—Was that where DNA can get transferred here on meteorites or something?

—Close enough.

—Why aren't you studying this stuff? It's important.

—Panspermia is concerned with how life-forms are distributed throughout space, but I'm more interested in abiogenesis—that is, the origin of life.

—Whatever. I guess I have no say in the matter.

—I'll tell you what, if you bring me an alien, I'll take it to our lab and compare its genome to the human genome. Maybe then we'll have a definitive answer.

—Now you're just making fun of me. You're mean.

—Where's *your* sense of humor?

—It's not a joke.

—Okay, I'm serious. If you have a source, I'll make the alien genome project my next PhD thesis.

—Me? Get it yourself. The government has aliens in a warehouse out in Vegas.

—Huh? I don't think so.

—What's it called? Area 51 or something.

—Area 51 is an air force test facility, not an alien storage facility.

—How can you be so sure they aren't testing aliens? Since you work for NASA, you should ask around. Maybe you can get in there. That would be awesome.

—Very funny. I'm a scientist, not a conspiracy theorist.

—But you said earlier that aliens probably existed.

—I didn't say on Earth.

—Why not Earth? It's possible, isn't it?

—Well, if it will make you feel better. It's possible. We have meteorite fragments that contain traces of extraterrestrial proteins. We have others that contain carbon-based compounds like sugars and amino acids. Perhaps someday someone will prove the seeds of the human race were of extraterrestrial origin. Are you happy now?

—Really? How can we prove that right now?

—Like I said, if you bring me an alien, I can perform an analysis comparing human DNA with the extraterrestrial DNA.

—So, we're right back where we started?

—Welcome to science.

—I'm beginning to hate science.

—Science is your friend. Why fight it?

—The problem with science is that it's limited to things that can be measured.

—Yes, you mentioned that. We thrive on repeatable experiments.

—That's true.

—Science continually develops new tools to measure and quantify natural phenomena.

—The most interesting things about life can't be measured.

—The list of things we can measure grows every day.

—I still think your lack of interest in art is odd.

—It's odd to me that more people aren't interested in space exploration.

—How often do you think about typography?

—Typography? You mean typeface design?

—Yeah, like fonts and stuff.

—Never.

—Exactly. I bet in all the hours you've spent typing your Martian thesis thingy you never once thought about the origin of the font you're using.

—Very true. And your point?

—You stared at that page for hours and never saw the letters. You only cared about the ideas.

—Point taken.

—If you were interested in the letters, you'd know the name of the font and its history. Who designed it? Is it a serif or sans serif font?

—Why do you think more people aren't interested in space exploration?

—Because most people are just trying to make it through the day. They want to finish the report and go home. They don't care about typography.

—Perhaps.

—Do you think about who made your clothes? How did the worker feel that day as they sewed the collar onto your shirt?

—I don't think about stuff like that.

—Why not?

—Perhaps I'm just trying to make it through the day. Perhaps I'm just not interested. We can't think about everything. We have to choose.

—I use a microwave every day and I have no idea how it works.

—An electromagnetic field causes the water molecules to vibrate and create molecular friction, thus producing heat.

—The reason I don't know is because I'm not interested.

—You can't ignore physics. It's everywhere. It's the relationship between energy and matter. We use it all the time. How you apply brakes in your car. How soon? How much pressure? A gasoline-powered car is powered by a rhythm of explosions.

—I don't drive.

—Fine.

—What about books?

—*What* about books?

—Do you read?

—That's all I do.

—No, no. I mean fiction.

—We already discussed art.

—You should read novels. It makes you more empathetic.

—You think I need more empathy?

—Don't we all?

—That's a question of values.

—How can you not enjoy a good story?

—I'm not interested in fiction.

—Why is that?

—Do I need to justify my lack of interest in something?

—Yes.

—I don't feel a need to justify my preferences.

—Fiction helps you understand reality and our place in it.

—Who made you an authority on reality?

—Don't you want to learn about yourself?

—No.

—Why not?

—I'm not that interesting.

—And Mars is?

—Of course. That's why it's my life's work.

—There's something you're not telling me.

—I'd rather not talk about it.

—I'm just asking. Are all your opinions classified like your alien research?

—Okay, apparently suspension of disbelief is difficult for me. I don't enjoy fiction because I'm distracted by inconsistencies in the story. Fiction asks me to intentionally shut off my ability to analyze. I don't like that.

—I can see that. You're too analytical. Being analytical prevents you from enjoying nonsense. I love nonsense.

—Nonsense? I have no interest in nonsense.

—I feel sorry for people who don't like nonsense.

—Why?

—Because it's everywhere.

—I feel sorry for people who like nonsense.

—It's sad you can't enjoy nonsense.

—You're funny.

—You're looking for answers under rocks on Mars. Does that make any sense?

[He laughs and then she laughs.]

—It does to me. I don't expect you to understand.

—You've spent your whole life trying to make sense of everything, and what has it got you?

—Several degrees. And soon a PhD. Is that enough?

—Maybe appreciating nonsense could help you understand those quantum theories you find so confusing.

—You think quantum theory is nonsense?

—As you know, it could be proven wrong someday. Lots of *sciencey* stuff has been proven wrong.

—*Sciencey* is not a word.

—It is now. Where do you think words come from? Our ancestors just made them up.

—I think you overestimate your ability to be irrational.

—Funny, I think you overestimate your ability to be rational.

—Are you suggesting that I delude myself?

—Don't we all? Life isn't easy for anyone.

—Sure. We all tend to fall prey to confirmation biases. I try to improve my cognition every day. I want to learn every day.

—The difference between us is you're trying to learn something every day, and I'm trying to unlearn something every day.

—Unlearning? I'm just about to get a PhD, so unlearning is not an option for me right now.

—I see. Maybe you can consider it in the future. Like after you get your PhD.

—What does that even mean? How does one *unlearn* something?

—It's all about programing! We were kids minding our business, and society comes along and beats the innocence out of us. Children live in a world of infinite possibilities until the government programs us to be corporate drones that don't ask questions. We were wild horses until they reined us in.

—Perhaps. Asking too many questions has definitely gotten me into trouble over the years.

—Asking questions eventually reveals the truth.

—I'm glad my profession supports asking questions.

—Yep, scientists and artists get some leeway in our society to be subversive.

—Perhaps, but I don't see myself as a subversive.

—Trust me, you're a subversive. You challenge your brain. And society.

—Is that so? Why do you say that?

—Asking questions is subversive. It challenges the status quo.

—There are limits to our cognition.

—Are you saying I don't control my brain?

—Hardly. Most of our processing is unconscious. Our brain is overwhelmed, so it looks for shortcuts to cope. These shortcuts are cognitive biases. Look it up.

—And scientists are immune to this disease?

—Of course not, scientist fall prey all the time. They too want to find simple explanations for natural phenomena.

—I don't blame them. Simple solutions are the best.

—For instance, the unified field theory attempts to describe the behavior of all fundamental forces and elementary particles in a single mathematical equation. Some call it the theory of everything.

—I like Oneness, so that sounds good. Is that even possible to do in one math problem?

—The challenge is that it may be a futile attempt to oversimplify a vastly complex universe.

—Okay, this is hurting my brain. We should play a game.

—No thanks. I don't like games.

—You'll like this one. It's called the pocket game. We pull out what's in our pockets and whoever has the most interesting thing wins.

—Okay, I have just the thing.

[He pulls out a small, rocklike object and places it on the table in front of her.]

—Am I supposed to be impressed by this rock?

—Pick it up. It's a meteorite.

—Really? From outer space?

[She picks it up and rubs it against her cheek.]

—Wow, this came from outer space?

—Sure. It burned through the atmosphere, so you can't damage it.

—Wow, it's small but heavy.

—Yes, it's an extraterrestrial object. I thought you'd like it.

—Why is it so heavy?

—It's classified as an iron meteorite, which are relatively dense. Its composition is approximately ninety-three percent iron, with traces of other metallic elements.

—That's quite a journey for this little guy. He survived a flight through space, blasting through the atmosphere, and a crashing into the earth.

—This is just a small piece of a larger meteor. It exploded into a fireball when it collided with Earth's atmosphere— that's called an airburst. The remaining fragments fell to the earth—those are called meteorites.

—Fireball? You mean a shooting star?

—Yes, shooting star, in the vernacular.

—Why do things explode when they get near Earth?

—Do you really want to hear about the frictional super-heating of hypersonic objects?

—No, not when you put it that way. Maybe you can put it in layperson's terms.

—Perhaps I can simplify it. When a meteor hits our atmosphere the air in front of it becomes highly compressed, changing its kinetic energy into heat. The tremendous heat causes the object to glow and disintegrate. That's what you call a shooting star.

—That's the simple version?

—It's just friction. Haven't you heard of friction?

—Sure, like how your hands heat up when you rub them together.

—This meteorite is from the 1947 Sikhote-Alin meteorite shower in Russia. Have you heard of it?

—No, why would I?

—Because it was the largest meteorite shower in modern times!

—Sorry, I'm not really up on my meteorite shower history.

—I'm sorry. I'll stop talking. I know I can get carried away.

—Why do we know so much about this? I'm sure there's a story.

—Actually, there is a story. Since it happened during the day, many people witnessed the massive explosion. One of the witnesses was a local artist who saw the fireball while he sat at his window preparing to work.

—I should have known there was an artist involved.

—He immediately began a sketch that became a well-known painting documenting the fireball and smoke trail.

—So artists have some value?

—I didn't say they didn't.

—Can I have it?

—No, but you can buy your own online. They're relatively common, so they're inexpensive.

[He grabs it from her hand and shoves it in his pocket.]

—How old is that thing?

—Hard to say exactly, but it's in the millions.

—Millions?

—Maybe hundreds of millions.

—Wow, that's really, really, really old.

—Relatively old. Earth is approximately 4.5 *billion* years old.

—Is everything in space *billions* of years old?

—Not everything. The light from the stars we see may only be a million years old.

—Wait, a million years old? So when I'm looking at the night sky the light I see is really old light?

—Yes, the light you see may even be from stars that no longer exist.

—Wow, I can't get my head around that. So when we look into space we're looking back in time?

—Yes, back in time.

—It's funny that we associate outer space stuff with the future when everything in space is ancient.

—I blame science fiction for that.

—Time is weird. I wonder why we have it. Have you thought about that?

—Ray Cummings said the purpose of time is to prevent everything from happening at once.

—That makes total sense. To separate events.

—It's all relative. Pun intended.

—Good one.

—It's your turn.

—What do you mean?

—What's in your pocket?

—I don't have any pockets. You win!

—Let me get this straight. You initiated this so-called *pocket* game fully aware that you had no pockets?

—How else was I supposed to find out what was in your pockets?

—You're a strange little bird.

—Thank you.

—Was that a compliment?

—I take everything as a compliment.

—Why?

—It makes it easier to like people.

—I'll have to try that.

—People only insult you when they're afraid of your power.

—Interesting theory. I'll take that under advisement.

—Can I hold the meteorite again?

—No, you've had enough.

—Why not?

—Because I don't trust you to return it.

—But I want to feel its energy again.

—Energy?

—Yes, it's alive. You feel it too. That's why you carry it with you.

—What are you talking about?

—I told you everything is alive.

—Yes, you mentioned that before. It's called panpsychism.

—Right. Panpsychism. I don't understand why you're so dismissive of that idea.

—I don't dismiss it. I just have no way of testing that theory.

—I see. So we're back to measuring things?

—If it makes you feel better, we have a Martian meteorite that appears to contain fossilized evidence of ancient bacteria.

—What? Are you saying that alien life-forms can fly through space and land here?

—Yes. Didn't I mention that?

—So it can survive being burned up in the atmosphere?

—Apparently, that's the case. Experiments have been conducted where bacterial DNA was applied to the exterior of spacecraft, and the DNA remained viable even after reentry through our atmosphere.

—Wow, I have a lot of questions. I need details.

—Maybe I can answer them.

—How does a rock leave a planet?

—Most commonly through volcanic activity.

—So it just gets blasted into space?

—Correct.

—And it just lands here by chance?

—According to you, everything is conscious, so maybe it steers itself here.

—True. But it could just be random?

—More than likely.

—So, how do we know it was from Mars?

—Well, to put it simply, the two Viking spacecraft have produced significant amounts of data about the Martian atmosphere. The abundance of rare isotopes trapped in the meteorite matches those in the Martian atmosphere. This correlation makes it highly probable that the meteorite is of Martian origin.

—Interesting. So this probably happened on other planets too.

—Perhaps.

—So now we know how alien life spreads all over the universe.

—Perhaps.

—Well, thank you. You've given me lots to think about.

—Well, thank you for your interest. Are you leaving?

—I was about to . . . Don't you want to get back to your work?

—I can spare a few more minutes.

—Okay . . . Do you live here in Pasadena?

—Yes, and you?

—Me too. I live in an old Victorian house up on Orange Grove. It's easy to imagine I'm living the bohemian life in a Parisian garret during the Belle *Époque*, with all the arts flourishing around me.

—No heating or air-conditioning. Dying of tuberculosis. No thank you. Why romanticize that?

—I know the reality of life then was not as romantic as it's portrayed, but you don't have to ruin it for me.

—Sorry. It sounds perfect for you.

—It is perfect for me. And as an added bonus, there are ghosts.

—So you believe in ghosts? Of course you do. Why am I not surprised?

—They mess with the electricity and move stuff around.

—I'm sure there's a logical explanation.

—Yes, the logical explanation is there are ghosts.

—And you're not afraid?

—Afraid of ghosts? Why should I be afraid? I find it life-affirming.

—Ghosts are life-affirming?

—Of course. You need life to have death, and death to have life.

—That's true. Cycle of life.

—Maybe I lived in Paris in a past life. Have you been?

—To Paris? Yes, I went on a side trip after visiting CERN in Switzerland.

—CERN? That's the big tunnel thingy that smashes things together?

—Exactly. I'm impressed you've heard of it.

—Tell me what stands out. What do you remember about Paris?

—About Paris? I remember a lot of loose dogs and the resulting excrement.

—That's it? Dog poop? That's all you remember? Did you happen to notice any architecture or art? Or a big tower? The Eiffel Tower!

—Of course I saw those things, but you asked me what stood out.

—I don't want to talk about dog poop. I want to talk about art and architecture and culture.

—That stuff didn't stand out to me because it looked just the way I expected it to look. The Eiffel Tower looks just the way it does in the pictures. The *Mona Lisa* looks exactly like the numerous reproductions.

—You've been to Paris and you still don't understand art. Paris was wasted on you. What a tragedy.

—Here we are discussing art again. What can I say? I have nothing to contribute.

—Humans will never stop talking about art. It's what makes us human.

—I understand art. I just don't place as high a value on it as you do.

—If you think an imitation is as good as an original, you definitely don't understand art.

—Okay, okay. Let me tell you what it was like to see the *Mona Lisa.* Mind you, I only went because it's the most famous painting in the world. I was hoping to learn what the fuss was all about. After waiting in line for hours, I was funneled into the museum with a crowd of tourists. After finally getting in front of the painting, there was a barrage of continuous flash photography that obscured the painting. After a few seconds the line moved on. I would describe the experience as anticlimactic.

—I can't believe it. That sounds horrible. No wonder you didn't like it.

—Fifteen seconds. That's how long the average visitor views the painting.

—How sad. What a shame.

—So that's why I suggest a *Mona Lisa* reproduction.

—Well, I'm still planning to go, and I'm still expecting it to be a religious experience.

—Even after my description?

—You had the wrong mindset. I'm sure I'll appreciate it more than you did.

—I had no expectations going in. I feel no obligation toward the *Mona Lisa*. I was open to the experience and I was disappointed. Not sure what the big deal is.

—This is how important that painting is. In 1911 the *Mona Lisa* was stolen from the Louvre. As authorities all over the world searched for it, visitors continued to stand in line to see the empty wall where the painting had been. The empty wall!

—That doesn't surprise me. Tourists are irrational. They'll stand in line for anything.

—It's not fair that *you've* been to Paris and I haven't.

—I've heard life isn't fair. It's not fair you're charming and I'm not.

—Ha! Good one. Thanks for the compliment.

—You're welcome. Well, if you want to talk about art, I have some questions.

—Bring it on.

—Why do the nude models from that era seem so depressed?

—I regret bringing up nudity. You seem fixated on it.

—Too bad. You started it.

—Fine. Many models in that era were courtesans.

—Prostitutes?

—We call them *sex workers* now. Unknown artists had a hard time hiring professional models, so they had to make other arrangements. Life was a struggle for everybody, especially the poor. Especially poor artists.

—So you're saying a lack of resources informed their artistic choices.

—Exactly. These paintings may be in museums now, but at that time they were worthless.

—That's difficult to imagine, since some of those impressionist paintings are now worth millions.

—Yep, it's a cruel joke the universe played on those artists. Van Gogh sold only one painting in his lifetime. And his brother was an art dealer!

—It seems odd to see all those nudes in those museums when the rest of the world was so prudish at the time. Why wasn't that controversial?

—Paris was liberal, so nudity didn't shock people. They were controversial because of the politics.

—Nude paintings have political implications?

—Of course. Context is everything in art. Everything is political. That's where the meaning comes from.

—So you're saying the environment the work is created in has an impact on how the work is received?

—Of course. Isn't everything like that? Context is huge. It includes the artist's background as well as historical, political, philosophical, and cultural stuff.

—I see. So it was an act of rebellion?

—You could say that. Even though sex work was common then, it was still taboo. These paintings brought courtesans from the fringes of society into the mainstream.

—So polite society was confused.

—Audiences were not shocked by the nudity but by their bold attitudes. Women in those times were expected to be meek and submissive, but these women stared back at you from the canvas. That's why they were controversial.

—I see. So social mores were being challenged?

—Yep, this was the beginning of the women's suffrage movement.

—That's where the *political* implications come in.

—Lots of things were changing at the time. New technologies, like photography, liberated art.

—It's hard to imagine photography as high-tech.

—Yep, a lot has changed since then.

—How was photography a liberating force?

—Before photography, painting was used to document the elite and their stuff. Paintings were status symbols commissioned by royalty, churches, and aristocrats. You know, to show off power and wealth.

—You're talking about portraiture?

—Since photography was better at documenting things, it took over. Artists could now do whatever they wanted. They were free to express themselves. Artists challenged the status quo and became celebrities.

—Self-expression instead of commission work.

—Art was celebrated for its own value.

—Art for art's sake?

—Exactly.

—Okay, enough art talk.

—Speaking of prostitutes—I mean sex workers, I just remembered a story. May I?

—Only if it's *not* about art.

—Okay, I'll give you a break from art. One day, I was at home practicing standing still—

—Wait, you have to practice that?

—That's not important right now. Just listen.

—Sorry.

—I heard a knock at the door, and when I opened it, there was an old man standing there. He said he was visiting from Ohio and asked to come inside. Of course I said hell no. He said he was in love with a prostitute—his word—

who lived there during the war, meaning World War II. He could tell I didn't believe him, so he went on to describe my room in shocking detail. He said he would visit her in the afternoon, and they would stay in bed for hours. He said at a certain time of day a shaft of sunlight would come in and hit the crystal doorknob on the closet door and flecks of rainbow colors would magically scatter about the room. I knew that magic, so I let him in. He sat on my bed silently for a few minutes, looking out the window. A tear came into his eye. He rubbed his face and got up and left. I never saw him again.

—Interesting. I don't think I'd let a stranger into my house.

—He wasn't a stranger. He was a kindred spirit. My question to you is: Does anything weird like that happen to you?

—No.

—How sad.

—I don't feel the need to seek out *weird* experiences.

—What about dreams? Do you have weird dreams?

—I don't remember my dreams.

—Really? I have bizarre dreams. Sometimes they're abstract. I want to remember them, so I keep a dream journal. It helps you remember, but you have to do it first thing in the morning.

—How do you document an *abstract* dream?

—I write down any colors, shapes, or feelings that come up. You should keep a dream journal. It'll help you remember your dreams.

—I think it's good that I don't remember them anymore.

—Why?

—They're probably nightmares about my anxieties associated with my thesis. Or data analysis.

—Wouldn't that be good to know? Don't you want to know what's going on in your subconscious mind?

—No, I don't like dreams. They don't make sense.

—That's why I love them!

—Why do you like dreams so much?

—I enjoy the freedom.

—Freedom?

—Only in dreams do we have full creative control. Where else can we transcend the boundaries of logic and time?

—Not interested.

—Okay, let's talk about science. Dreams are important. They give you helpful insights into your subconscious mind.

—Are you saying dreams have practical applications?

—Of course. You can use them to solve problems. You can ask yourself questions before you fall asleep and wake up with answers.

—Has this been the subject of any scientific studies?

—I don't know. Science is your problem.

—I've never heard of it before.

—Who's that guy who drew that carbon ring thingy?

—Carbon rings? Did you just reference Friedrich Kekulé? Why do you know him?

—I can read!

—He discovered that benzene molecules are made of rings of carbon atoms.

—Yes! That's it. He got that from a dream. He fell asleep in front of the fireplace. The sparks turned into dancing molecules and then turned into a snake, and then it ate its own tail!

—I find that hard to believe.

—Look it up.

—I intend to.

—Oh, what's that table thingy with all the elements and stuff?

—Are you referring to the periodic table?

—Yeah! Who's that guy?

—Mendeleev.

—The layout of the elements came to him in a dream.

—Huh. I must admit that does sound familiar.

—There're lots of examples. Indigenous cultures are more interested in dreams, but we've lost touch with that world. I think it's sad. Maybe it'll come back someday.

—I intend to look into this.

—Really? You're more open-minded than I thought.

—Just because I'm skeptical doesn't mean I can't evolve.

—The universe doesn't care about your skepticism.

—I can see that.

—There's a part of you that's always awake. That's why you remember your dreams.

—Perhaps.

—But I hate it when dream emotions spill into my waking life.

—How so?

—A few nights ago I dreamed I was a mortician and my business partner died. His evil children forced me out of the business, and I lost everything. I'm still mad about that.

—You take this quite seriously.

—One time I dreamed a close friend betrayed me, and I was mad about that for days. I had to keep reminding myself that it was just a dream. Just a dream. Just a bad dream.

—I can see how that could be problematic.

—Sometimes it's hard to know if the dream is good or bad.

—Must you decide?

—Years ago I had a dream where I was standing in a field and it began to rain like crazy.

—Was that a bad dream?

—No, I was a farmer, and the rain ended a long drought.

—So it was a good dream?

—I thought so until I was struck by lightning.

—So it was bad?

—It hit my right shoulder, shot down my leg, and knocked my boot off. It just went flying into the air as I fell to the ground. When I stood up again I realized my persistent back pain was gone. It was a miracle!

—So it was good?

—Sure, I guess we can call that one a good dream.

—That one was very dramatic.

—It was especially vivid. I can still smell the fertilizer.

—You have smells in your dreams?

—Of course. I thought everyone did.

—I don't think so, but I can't be sure.

—Oh, I just remembered another good one. I had this very vivid dream where my only mode of transportation was a unicycle. The seat was really tall and it was scary to ride. It was something like a circus clown would ride. That was definitely a bad dream.

—I hate the circus.

—Me too. I feel bad for the animals.

—Me too.

—My dreams are so vivid that it takes me a while to figure out who I am when I wake up in the morning.

—Well, that sounds problematic.

—It's more of an inconvenience than anything. I just have to wait in bed until I remember what I'm supposed to be doing. I remember I am human. What do humans do? What's my job? It slowly returns to me, this life. I'm just billions of molecules getting together to be me for this lifetime.

—I'm glad I don't have that problem.

—It's especially confusing when I wake up in the middle of a dream where I'm someone else.

—Sounds like you have quite the nightlife.

—Tonight I'll probably dream I'm a socially awkward astrobiologist sitting in a coffeehouse working on a thesis about Martians . . .

[*Ding. Ding. Ding.* The alarm on her phone goes off and she scrambles to silence it.]

—Well, as you can see this concludes our time together. It was nice chatting with you. Good luck with your thesis thingy. I need to get back to work.

[She stands up and salutes him.]

—Wait . . . well . . . um . . .

—Yes?

—Well . . . will I see you again?

—How should I know? I'm just a pawn in the game of life.

—Are we talking about the same thing?

—Everything has a beginning, middle, and end. That's what makes a story.

—I didn't know there was . . . an end.

—Besides, you know too many of my secrets.

[He looks sad and confused.]

—But what if I . . . would want to see you again? How could I make that happen?

—It's too late, because I've already told you my secrets.

—I'm confused.

—You see, realizing there's always an end is the best way to appreciate the present. I'm sorry you're not satisfied.

—But I thought this was the beginning. How could I know it was the end?

—Have you heard of the mayfly?

—Of course. They are known for their relatively short life span. Why?

—A mayfly lives only for a day. It emerges from the water, dances, mates, lays eggs, and dies. A complete cycle of life in just a few hours.

—I see. You mean like us.

—Just like us.

—I don't know what to say.

—Say you love coffee and sunshine.

—I love coffee and sunshine.

[She straightens her bathrobe and starts toward the door.]

—The time to enjoy the dance is while you are dancing.

Acknowledgements

I'm beyond grateful to everyone on the Unnamed Press and Rare Bird Literary teams for teaching me the ropes and bringing this book to life. Special thanks to Chris Heiser for believing in me, Tyson Cornell for entertaining my half-baked ideas, Allison Miriam Smith for her eternal patience, Jaya Nicely for the beautiful cover, Mike McNamara for all the good cheer, Ian Byers-Gamber for the author photo and Halley Parry and Nancy Tan for their editorial expertise.

I would like to express my deepest appreciation to the following wordsmiths and colleagues for their ongoing support and inspiration: Mark Haskell Smith, Hector Tobar, Chip Jacobs, Paula Johnson, Katayoon Zandvakili, J. Ryan Stradal, Steve Salardino, David Shook and Joel Arquillos.

Finally, I would be remiss in not acknowledging the unwavering support of my family and friends, especially my parents. Without your love, advice and inspiration I would be nothing. I can't thank you enough.

Printed in the USA
CPSIA information can be obtained
at www.ICGtesting.com
JSHW020435020823
45798JS00003B/17